DERANGED

Borgo Press Books by LONNI LEES

Deranged: A Novel of Horror

DERANGED

A NOVEL OF HORROR

LONNI LEES

THE BORGO PRESS

MMXI

DERANGED

FIRST EDITION

Published by Wildside Press LLC

www.wildsidebooks.com

DEDICATION

To *Nancy Skinner Nordhoff*, founder of Hedgebrook Writer's Retreat for Women on Whidbey Island, Washington, for her encouragement and friendship and selfless support. And to *Hedgebrook*, for their precious and priceless gifts of time and inspiration and solitude.

To my husband, *Jonathan DuHamel*, for showing his love by building me a room of my own.

And to the memory of *Donna F.*, a young victim who did not survive.

CONTENTS

PROLOGUE

"Often the test of courage is not to die but to live."
—Conte Vittorio Alfieri

Charlie Blackhawk drove the silver 1979 Nova with his left hand on the wheel and his right hand around the cold can of beer planted between his legs. Its coolness against his thighs felt good. The small finger of his right hand absent-mindedly rubbed against his crotch as he hummed along to an old Waylon Jennings song on the radio. The day had hardly begun, but he was already getting itchy and restless.

Forty minutes had passed since Charlie had last seen another car along the deserted stretch of road. The main road had too many trucks and too many drunks heading to or from Las Vegas, so he'd picked up the secondary road at Jean, Nevada and was driving along the dusty, isolated route that passed through Nipton on the California side.

Charlie had already sped through Ivanpah, Cima, and Kelso, blurs on a forgotten map of nowhere. He drove along an empty stretch of desert called the Devil's Playground. It's got a nice ring to it, Charlie thought to himself as he hummed off-key to a honky-tonk instrumental playing on the car radio. He planned to pick up U.S. 91 again when he reached his gas stop in Barstow.

Charlie felt himself getting hard beneath the Levis where his hand rested. He jerked his hand away, nearly spilling the can of beer.

"I wasn't being bad, Momma. I wasn't doin' nothing bad."

He spat out the words through clenched teeth.

Charlie pulled the Nova to the shoulder of the road, still mumbling to himself. He turned off the key and pushed open the door. Pacing along the length of the car, he uttered words that had meaning only to himself while he kicked the desert sand with his boots. Charlie was six-foot-one, tanned, and well-built. He had a rugged, outdoors man look about him with a chiseled face that hid his dark intentions.

This morning's beer was begging for release from Charlie's full bladder. His boots crunched the sand along the desert floor. He paused, unzipped his pants. Steam rose as he pissed a sunning lizard off its resting place on a rock, sending it scurrying to safer ground. Urine streamed down the rock, collecting in hot puddles on the ground.

Charlie laughed.

Paiute Wells was behind him.

That little hell-hole of a town had managed to bore him to death in less than a month. Nothing happened there. Nothing that would go unnoticed, so Charlie was itching for some action. So far, 1990 was proving to be a good year. He had been working his way back to California for the last three months, stopping off here and there to work for enough pocket money to keep him going. It was easy to find some dive or greasy spoon that was happy to pay a hungry drifter cash under the table. For half the going wage. He had figured that out years ago. But they didn't ask questions and he left no footprint. Like he'd never been there. Like he was invisible. Like he was nobody at all.

It was time to head back to the cabin. He walked back to the car, guzzled the remaining beer, and tossed the empty can to the floor.

He reached across the seat for his Camel Filters, pulled one from the pack, and lit it. He drew the soothing smoke into his lungs, then exhaled as he turned the key in the ignition, stepped on the gas and returned to the road.

Driving along the desolate stretch of highway, Charlie's mind drifted like the desert sands...from past to present and back again. It was a trick that his thoughts liked to play on him—taking him back, each time pulling ugly little pieces of that past and wedging them into the present. Sometimes Charlie drifted so deeply into the fogbank of mental trickery that he lost all concept of time and space. More often than not he was unaware of the retrogressions.

Three miles farther down the road, Charlie spotted the twisted wreckage.

He slowed to forty, then thirty, then to a crawl as he pulled up behind the mangled cars. They were a black Mercedes and an old Dodge and judging by appearances they'd hit head on. A New Mexico license plate hung loosely from the back bumper of the Mercedes. The front end was pushed in and the left fender was crushed against the Dodge.

There was a young woman slumped behind the wheel of the Mercedes. Her head had fallen forward and long blonde hair partially covered her face.

She was not moving.

As he walked up to the dented door on the driver's side he saw the blood trickling from her ear, sunlight flickering along its path—bright and shiny and beautiful. One eye was dislodged from its socket.

He'd be back.

He turned and walked to the Dodge and looked inside. The man who had been driving was thrown to the passenger's side, his skull crushed where it must have slammed against the metal of the door.

He was dead.

No problem there.

Charlie returned to his own car and reached in for his keys. He walked around to the back and opened the trunk, pushing aside several license plates that lay among his clothing and other belongings. Removing a screwdriver from his tool kit he then walked around to the back of the Mercedes.

Crouching down, Charlie began to unscrew the license plate.

He heard a faint moan from inside the car.

Ignoring it, Charlie finished loosening the license plate, stood up and walked slowly back to his car. He whistled as he walked, then threw the license and the screwdriver into the trunk and walked over to the passenger side of the Dodge.

The door was jammed.

Charlie held the handle and pushed away from the car with his left foot while he pulled with all his strength on the handle. It finally gave way with a loud, creaking moan. The body fell, its arm and what was left of its head thudding to the ground.

Rifling through the man's pockets, Charlie finally found what he sought. He opened the wallet and counted the money that it held. Seventy-two dollars. Charlie took sixty dollars and pushed the wallet back into the dead man's pocket. He grabbed the corpse under the arms and lifted it back to the seat. Brains, like a spilled bucket of earthworms, oozed from the crushed cranium. The blood was already clotting. Charlie kicked the door shut with his boot and spat on the ground.

He walked over to the Mercedes and tried the door. It was locked. Humming and smiling as he walked to the other side of the car, he then tried the door on the passenger's side.

The door opened.

The woman moaned although she didn't move.

"H...help...please," she stammered, almost inaudibly.

Charlie knew that look very well. She was dying. He didn't need a doctor or a paramedic or a fucking coroner to tell him *that!*

Charlie liked to watch things die, but he ignored her as his eyes searched the floor for her purse. He finally spotted it, sandwiched between the woman and the door. He grabbed a fistful of her hair and roughly pulled her head back. He reached across her slumped body and took the purse. He looked up at her bloody face—at the eyeball gutter balling across her cheek. Blood continued to trickle from her ears as she moaned. It was fun for Charlie to watch her—he was hypnotized by the tracks of blood that zigzagged across her face like a crazy road map, but he did not want to be distracted from his main objective. He had business to take care of and he didn't know how much time he had before another car might come along this road. It could be an hour or it could be five minutes. He returned his focus to her purse.

There was over seven-hundred dollars in cash along with several credit cards. He left the credit cards—they could be monitored and traced, if anyone figured out he'd been there, which was doubtful. Charlie was always careful. He never got caught. He was invisible. Nothing more than a phantom riding a dark wind. He took six-hundred and thirty dollars and shoved the remaining seventy back into the wallet. Not a hint of a crime. Not a clue anyone had been there.

"Didn't anyone ever tell you not to carry so much cash?" he whispered softly, as if to a lover. "Dumb, stupid bitch."

His tongue slowly traced the outline of her lips as she groaned. He lapped at the blood on her cheek. It tasted sweet and sticky and metallic as it danced across his taste buds. He flicked the eyeball with his finger and laughed as it rolled back and forth like a pendulum. Then he slid across the seat and was exiting the car when he spotted the small body in the back seat. It was a little girl about six or seven years old. Her neck appeared to be broken. She looked like a sleeping little Girl Scout in the pale green dress that was rumpled above her thighs.

She looked just like Lucy Mae. His sweet little sister from so very long ago.

He opened the back door and slid in. He put his arms around her, lifting her limp body and holding her close. Her head fell back. He hummed a lullaby as he rocked her in his arms.

Charlie Blackhawk was crying.

He laid the little girl back on the seat and watched her with sadness. The past melted into the present, confusing his thoughts.

"You murdering bitch!" Charlie yelled at the dying woman in the front seat, his screams assaulting the desert silence.

His calloused hand wiped angry tears from his face.

He reached for the girl. The feel of soft green fabric shot a current of electricity up his arm as he caressed it with his fingertips. His other hand toyed with the ruffle on her undies, exciting him, confusing him with mixed emotions. "I miss you Lucy," he whispered. "Please don't die." Gently, he removed the child's undies, rubbed them against his eyelids, then slipped them into his pocket. A part of him wanted her, another part longed to protect her. He wanted to protect the child but a darker force washed over him.

He inhaled deeply, then exhaled his fetid breath like a gust of wind from the depths of hell.

He sat up, leaned against the back of the seat and unzipped his fly.

It was time for the watching game.

That was when Charlie saw the car on the horizon.

The car that jolted him to the present with a thud. He judged it to be about five minutes away.

He reached for the handle on the car door. But the bitch in the front seat moaned. She was still alive. She was dying but she was still alive! What if she wasn't dead yet when the car reached the crash site? What if she could talk?

No problem.

No problem at all.

Charlie's strong hands reached toward the front seat. He grabbed the woman firmly by the head.

It was as easy as killing a chicken for a Sunday picnic.

No problem at all.

He walked casually back to his Nova and started the engine. He adjusted the rear-view mirror and pushed the dark, curly hair from his forehead.

Charlie's eyes were as grey as frozen smoke.

His car took off. Swirling clouds of dust devils danced in its wake as it headed for the gas stations and coffee shops of Barstow.

Charlie Blackhawk had worked up an appetite.

CHAPTER ONE

Spring was unpredictable, an inconstant season at best—a spoiled bitch who wouldn't make up her mind. In California, people rummaged through their closets for last year's bathing suits one day and reopened their umbrellas the next. Spring held her head with the defiance of a naughty child.

Hidden Meadows lay in a quiet valley forty miles north of Los Angeles, a graffiti-free Shangri-La, a place where bad things didn't happen. It was the unwritten clause in the escrow papers.

No smog—no urban blight—no problems.

But there is no idyllic meadow safe from the shadows cast by passing clouds.

Residents found false comfort in their illusions, for without the darkness there can be no light.

The day's weather was indecisive. Housewives debated turning on their pool heaters. By late afternoon clouds had pushed their way across the sky, forcing the early morning nip back into the air.

The rain began softly. By the middle of the night silver bullets of rain pinged against the darkened windows of the new two-story Colonial at 11 Avenida Larkspur. Rivulets formed in the contours of unsod dirt, their fingers coaxing mud from yard to gutter.

There was no moon.

An evil mist floated through the darkness as the rain tap-tap-tapped against the windows in an ominous monotone.

The night was black.

Amy woke up screaming.

It was the bad dream again. The same nightmare that woke her up last night and the night before. Once again, it was his face that had frightened her, staring at her with eyes that glowed cold like steel grey ball bearings. His face was the Gobi desert, deep wrinkled paths crisscrossing in an abstract pattern across his leathered skin.

Amy didn't know where he came from or why he frightened her so, but she knew that he was a threat—a terrible danger that her eleven-year-old mind was unable to comprehend. In the dream, the man would stand across the room and look at her. Just look at her with those cold grey eyes. He would not move. But he wouldn't stop staring either. He was scary. Now awake, Amy sat upright and cowered into the corner of her bed, pressing her back against the wall. Tiny trembling hands grasped the soft pink comforter and pulled it up around her face, leaving only her pale green eyes peering out into the darkness like a cowering fawn.

When she blinked, tears streamed down her cheeks, creating a silent, erratic pattern on the soft pink comforter held tightly against her face. She felt hot urine trickle onto her flannel pajama bottoms and couldn't make it stop.

She sobbed.

By the time Amy's father reached her room, her sobs had turned into frantic gasps. Her arms reached desperately toward his comforting presence.

The nightlight was all that kept the room from total darkness. Jerry Hamill stumbled across the room and sat on the bed. He put his arms around his daughter and held her tightly. She was damp with perspiration, her body trembling. Jerry released his hold and gently pushed her matted, pale red hair from her eyes. Even in the semi-darkness her eyes startled him. She was terrified. But of what? A nightmare?

Now fully awake, the horror still clung to her like a decomposing phantom. Her mind tried to push away the ghostly form whose menacing face continued to stare at her.

His was the face of the future.

Amy squeezed her eyes shut, trying desperately to erase his image as it etched itself against her closed lids. A horrified moan worked its way up from deep inside her, along with the bile that burned like acrid lava along the passage of her throat. Swallowing and gasping, she clung tightly to her father. To the safety she always felt in his arms.

Something was wrong. She knew that something was terribly wrong with her. There had always been the dreams. As far back as she could remember. The kind of dreams that were so real she could have sworn that they were the worst reality imaginable—the kind that left her disoriented and frightened upon awakening. At those times she would just lie there, unscrambling the images in her head until she was sure that it had, indeed, been only a dream.

A very bad dream.

There were also those that she dreamed when she was wide awake. On one level they were even worse. It had taken her a long time to realize what was happening. Sometimes she remembered them. Sometimes she was only aware of a time lapse. Occasionally, in school, she would find the other children staring at her. Or whispering. Or pointing at her, laughing. Then she knew that it had happened again—that she had blurted out some kind of nonsense—that the kids looked at her as if they thought she was crazy. Each episode gave them one more reason to laugh at her; one more reason to tease and taunt.

One more reason to label her *different*.

The dreams and images had not actually terrorized her until recently. Before, they had only been pictures, spontaneous splashes that some unknown artist had brushed across her mind. At times they were beautiful. Sometimes they were brief spurts—an unkempt garden bordered by bushes of bright orange geraniums—a meaningless exchange of unfamiliar words.

But the words!

At times the sentences staggered from her mouth like drunken sailors to the shock of herself and those around her. Bad words. Words that Amy would never have used. Dirty words.

But now, now the visions had taken on the face of terror and for the first time she was truly frightened. Control was slipping, sliding like heavy snow down a mountain slope. An avalanche that was roaring down a distant recess of her mind.

The bad man had disappeared, not all at once, but in an ecto-plasmic fog that spun and drifted, slowly dissipating in a malevolent zephyr that blew straight from the mouth of hell, until finally all traces of him were sucked into the darkness.

It had drained her, leaving her exhausted.

Jerry saw the dark circles that had painted themselves below Amy's eyes. His brow furrowed in worry and concern as he held her. He tucked the comforter around his daughter and it reminded him of the pink blanket she had been wrapped in the day he brought her home. A fragile bundle—a little bird with no feathers, fighting so hard for life. She had won life's first battle, but to this day remained a delicate child. Even now she was more the size of a seven-year-old than an eleven-year-old nearing another birthday.

He had always loved Amy. Loved her more than his own life. More than his own wife...*EX*-wife.

Jerry held Amy close, whispering reassurances, soothing her, holding her patiently in his arms until he finally felt her elfin form relax. He continued to hold his little girl long after her breathing slowed to the steady, undisturbed rhythm of sleep. He stayed with her through the night, protecting her from the unnamed darkness.

CHAPTER TWO

Charlie Blackhawk felt restless as he sat in the booth at the Barstow Coffee Shop. He shifted his weight, fidgeted with the salt and pepper shakers, traced the icy sweat from the sides of his water glass. It felt like an eternity had passed by the time the waitress finally sat the plate down in front of him. He scowled up at her, resisting the temptation to scold her for her incompetence as he mentally threw her to the floor and kicked the stupid right out of her. She ignored the dirty look he gave her, chomped on her gum, turned and walked away. Charlie looked down at the limp, greasy fries and began to eat. They were already half cold and were devoid of even the slightest hint of flavor. Even the rancid taste of last week's lard would have been an improvement. So he doused them with more salt, then reached across the table and picked up the ketchup bottle, pouring half the contents onto his plate. He swirled some fries into the puddle of ketchup and shoved them into his mouth.

He still couldn't taste them.

He was distracted.

Something else kept drawing his attention. Something more important to Charlie than the cold, greasy slop on the plate in front of him. The hunger pains no longer mattered for he was feeling another, more urgent ache. An ache that made his head throb and twist, an ache that made his vision blur and turn dark as a black cat prowling the alleyways at midnight, an ache that made his body hurt like hell. *An ache he had to take care of.* That car crash on the road had stirred things up, made him bubble inside like a volcano building pressure before its inevitable explosion. And Charlie needed to explode. It was only mid-morning but he had already checked into a motel, knowing he had no choice but to take care of things before he could move on.

But there would be no truck stop lot lizards on the menu today. There was no time for negotiations with the hungry, nasty little whores that wove in and out between the semis in search of their mid-morning tricks. There was only time to feed his face—and assuage his other hunger—before moving on.

He finally got the waitress's attention and motioned her for the check. If she was running true to form her delivery would be slow as molasses. Damned if he would be leaving a tip. He should be getting a discount for lousy service. The lazy twat didn't earn squat. But the lack of a tip wasn't good enough, if he didn't tip her then she would figure he just forgot. He wanted her to *know* she was a fuckup. He wanted her to know he was in control. He reached into his pocket and pulled out his wallet, removing a worn piece of paper. Nothing important on it, just an old to-do list that was long ago done. He took a penny and dropped it into the water glass, then placed the paper over it. Quickly he turned it upside-down on the table, not spilling as much as a drop. An old trick but still a good one. It sent a definite message. He knew that when she went to lift the glass, the water would spill all over the place and she would have to clean up the mess. That would teach her not to fuck with Charlie Blackhawk. Too bad there was no time to *really* show her. He chuckled as he rose from the booth, walked to the register and paid his check with some of the dead man's cash. He pushed through the door and stood out front in the blinding light, his eyes scanning the street in both directions until he regained his bearings. He finally remembered where he was. He walked back to the motel and entered his room, closing the door behind him. He opened it again, putting the DO NOT DISTURB sign on the outside doorknob. Closed the door again. Locked it. Hooked the chain lock for good measure. Then he closed the drapes so not as much as a sliver of daylight could enter the darkened room.

So nothing could distract him.

His heart pounded as he stood in front of the mirror. He watched himself as he removed his clothing, staring at his naked reflection and at the little girl's undies clutched in his hand. He raised his hand, rubbed the small garment across his eyelids, caressed his cheekbones with it, inhaled deeply as it whispered past his nostrils.

It smelled of talc and laundry soap—and life.

She had been so young—so innocent—so helpless.

So...dead.

He stared at his reflection and smiled as his erection grew.

"You been a bad boy," he giggled.

He took the undies and knotted them around his penis, pulling the knot tighter and tighter until the pressure pinched into his flesh. He felt the pain shoot through his body, felt himself throb, pulsate, grow.

"Watch," Charlie whispered, grinning at the madman in the mirror.

CHAPTER THREE

Sabrina Stinson knocked on her neighbor's door until her knuckles hurt, cursing the broken doorbell, then knocked again. The bungalow was white, the old paint peeled and cracked, exposing deep gorges of dry-rot across its acned face. The entire neighborhood was decaying like Hollywood itself, stripped of pan stick and rouge—feeding on yesterday's illusions.

Sabrina shifted her weight impatiently. Intense eyes, the darkest of jade, peered through fiery locks of disheveled auburn hair. Her full, young lips signaled stubbornness and already hinted at her blossoming.

Cumulus clouds threatened the late afternoon sun. She knocked again on the door and kicked it impatiently with one worn jogging shoe. It hurt her toes.

"Shit," she mumbled.

Finally the door opened.

The old man looked down at Sabrina. His smile exposed dark gaps between his discolored teeth, and what hair remained on his head hung in greasy, unwashed strings of charcoal and yellowish-white. He smelled of garlic and pipe tobacco and the reek of menthol fumes from his linament.

"So where's the fire?" The old man asked.

"Didn't you hear me knocking?"

"If I didn't hear you, then I wouldn't be standing here, now would I?" he said, the faintest hint of an Eastern European accent in his voice.

"Sure, yeah," Sabrina mumbled, then remembering the old

man never wore his hearing aid she raised her voice and added: "I'll mow your lawn for only three bucks, but only if I can borrow the mower to do mine too."

"I don't think it really needs it, squirt."

"It always needs it, Mr. Owens," she said.

"Front and back?"

"Front." Sabrina knew the game. They played it every time. "The back'll cost you four bucks more. It's weed heaven back there and I always step in your stupid mutt's dog shit."

Despite her bluntness Sabrina liked Mr. Owens, especially as she could always pick up a few dollars from him for the movies without much trouble. The new Steven Seagal movie just opened on Hollywood Boulevard and if she hurried she could still make it to the early show—before the prices went up. She was anxious to see the movie. She loved Stallone and Chuck Norris and Charles Bronson. She liked Van Damme. And even Steven Seagal was okay in her book—despite the dumb pony tail there was nothing girlie or wishy-washy about him! Those guys really knew how to get the job done—they never took any shit from anybody. They were idealistic, determined, and tough as pig gristle. She admired them. They were her matinee idols.

Sabrina loved sitting in the darkened theaters all by herself, inhaling the aroma of stale popcorn and escaping within the fantasy world upon the screen. Her mother, Meggie, told her the same bug had bitten her when she was a teenager. Sabrina didn't mind the time alone while her mother pursued that dream. At the age of eleven Sabrina already realized that people had voids they needed to fill. After all, she had a few empty spaces of her own. If she had ever had a father, which her mother claimed she hadn't, it was nice to imagine him as looking like Chuck Norris. That was cool. Super cool. Norris was by far her all-time favorite and left the rest of them in the dust.

"Front and back?" Mr. Owens repeated.

"Front. It's getting late and I gotta mow mine too."

"Two dollars?"

"Three."

"What did you say?"

"Three!"

Sabrina was losing patience with his silly game—or was it his hearing? The game played out the same every time, but he always came through. She always won in the end. She liked winning.

Today she wanted to see the movie, then run over to the Hollywood Convalescent Home to visit Miss Cooney. Sabrina had been visiting the old woman often over the past months, ever since she had walked up to the front desk and said she was looking for an old lady with no relatives or friends left to visit with her. She told the nurse she wanted to adopt a grandmother. Someone she could tell stories to or maybe read to once in awhile. Or just listen to. Old people liked to talk about the past but no one really wanted to listen.

Shortly thereafter Meggie told Sabrina she had a real grandmother—somewhere—but despite Sabrina's prodding her mother was hesitant to commit to when they might meet. She wondered why her mother always seemed so guarded. About everything. For years Sabrina hadn't known a grandmother existed at all and now she just wanted to fill in the blanks. What was the big deal anyway?

So Miss Cooney remained her welcome surrogate. In the meantime they had become fast friends, eleven-year-old Sabrina and eighty-eight year old Miss Cooney. She looked forward to Sabrina reciting movie plots. Or reading her stories. Or just sitting there keeping her away from the loneliness. And sometimes Sabrina would sneak her an Oh Henry® if the nurses weren't around.

Old Miss Cooney loved her Oh Henry®'s.

"How would you like to make ten whole dollars?" Mr. Owens said.

Here it comes, she thought. Sabrina scowled at him, put her hands on her hips, planting her ragged shoes firmly on the wooden porch. She had a hard time suppressing a laugh.

"You're a silly old fart," she said. "Roboscout doesn't play those games." She had given herself that name after seeing Robocop and Robocop II. Roboscout. The strong sound of it appealed to her. She saw herself as a 'droid, too—half little girl scout and half virtuous tough guy. Just try to mess with that combo and see where it gets you!

"Just five minutes. Besides, Sugar Dumpling, you sure don't look as young as you are. It's a crime that a little gal like you can walk around looking so pretty. Hell, you look like Rita Hayworth, not Shirley Temple. Now Hayworth, there was a beauty. But you probably never heard of her—way, way before your time."

"Hey, I watch the late shows. I've seen *GILDA* three times!" The old pervert hit on her every time, but she knew he had a hard time just walking to the front door. It was impossible for her to imagine Mr. Owens ever having done "it". And he sure as hell wasn't capable of doing "it" now. One foot in front of the other and remembering to breathe was challenge enough for the old fart. It was just a harmless little game he liked to play with her, she knew that, but she warned him that if someone else overheard they might not understand at all.

"Walk up to the boulevard and you can find all the little girls you want. They're on every corner. This little girl just mows lawns."

"You drive a hard bargain, missy," he said, shaking his head. "The mower is on the side."

It played out the same every time—harmless banter, Sabrina knew that, but a little weird all the same.

Mr. Olsen pushed the greasy hair from his eyes, exposing the tattoo on his forearm. Sabrina looked at it, puzzled. It was nothing but numbers. No rose, no dagger, no "mom"—just a neat little row of numbers etched on old skin as thin as crepe paper.

"Why does your tattoo only have numbers? Is it so you don't forget your phone number or something?" she asked, knowing his memory tended to be foggy at times.

He hesitated before he spoke. "They gave it to me in the

camp. There was a time when all I was *was* a number. I keep it as a reminder of another life—when I was Solomon instead of Olsen."

"Camp? Like with canoes and counselors and stuff?"

He laughed at that, but she detected deep sorrow in his eyes. Camp was supposed to be a happy place.

"What?" She said.

"The world has a lot of dark places, little one. Some things are not for young girls with curious minds, or even for the ears of God."

He sighed and walked back into the house.

Sabrina shrugged, heard the front door creak shut as she walked to the side of the house and pushed to rusty mower down the driveway. The old geezer doing "it", just the thought made her giggle. Weeds crept up through cracked cement and ant hills dotted the walkway. She walked fast so the ants would not climb her ankles. It was difficult pushing the mower. It needed oiling and sharpening. It was as worn out as old Mr. Owens. She guessed living alone was making him senile. His wife had died long before Sabrina had become his neighbor. All he had left was his stinky pipe tobacco and that yapping little terrier.

Meggie had told her that men were totally useless and had nothing but sex on the brain. That was one tidbit of information she didn't keep under wraps. But even mom could not have imagined Mr. Owens thinking about "it". Did she not have a father because Meggie hated men so much? It seemed as if a family should have a father. And maybe a sister. Or a grandmother she could actually see and touch. But Sabrina had Meggie—and their roommate Betty—and as far back as she could remember, she had Buddy. She could talk to Buddy any time she wanted and Buddy was always there. Always had been, as far back as she could remember. Even though Buddy never answered back, she felt that she had someone with whom to share.

Buddy—the only thing she and her mother ever argued about. "You're too old for invisible playmates," her mother would say. "Make-believe friends are outgrown by the time kids are three or four. Just look at you, you're nearly a teenager and you cling to Buddy like an old security blanket." Her mother's voice was angry but her eyes were worried. Sabrina would tell her over and over again that Buddy wasn't make-believe, but a real girl kind of like herself—but tinier—and certainly sweeter. But even as she spoke she knew Meggie would never believe her. It did sound pretty stupid. Especially coming from a straight-A student who was supposed to be smart. But Buddy had always felt more real than imaginary. So Meg could only visualize a little pixie that Sabrina might pretend to hide in her pocket. But Buddy wasn't *that* tiny!

Hell, she needed Buddy.

Just as much as she needed old Miss Cooney.

Even more.

Because Buddy could share in her most private thoughts. Why, she could talk to Buddy about anything.

Sabrina pushed the mower through the tall grass and weeds and almost wished she had never started. Her muscles were starting to ache. She either had to stop using Mr. Olsen as her source of extra money or she had to do it a lot more often so it wasn't such an overwhelming job.

The mowing was almost impossible. But she was determined to keep up her end of the bargain. Once she set her mind to something, nothing would stop her.

She hung onto things with the determination and grip of a pit bull.

"Such willfulness," her mother would say. "I can't imagine where that comes from."

Maybe from my father, Sabrina wanted to say. But she knew that would start an argument...or make her mother uncomfortable. She tried to chose her words diplomatically in that area despite the fact that it gnawed at her.

A lot.

Sabrina dumped the lawn clippings in a heap against the side of Mr. Owen's garage, wiped the sweat from her face and headed home.

CHAPTER FOUR

Charlie Blackhawk's head was hurting again. It was hurting more lately, pushing to the surface memories best left buried and forgotten. Sometimes the voices made him cringe. Or cry. Or scream.

The Reverend Churchill's voice was blasting from the radio as it always did. Day and night. Winter and summer. Hallelulia! There was no music in the house, no news, no television, no books except a dusty old bible. Just the fucking Reverend Churchill yelling his non-stop threats of hell-fire and damnation and his fairy tale fantasies of repentance and the pearly gates of the great beyond. Little Charlie dared not cover his ears. That was blasphemy. Momma said so and Momma knew. She had driven the point home many times with a fist alongside his head—or a whack with an empty whiskey bottle that always left a big lump the size of an ostrich egg on his skull. Momma sure knew how to drive a point home effectively. Charlie gave her full credit for that. The Reverend was her savior and her salvation and had freed her from the devil's grasp. The same devil that had held her hand every night as she went to town in search of the comfort of strangers. The same devil that had cheered her on when she fornicated with nameless men behind seedy bars or dark alleyways or in the back seats of cars instead of seeking comfort and solace in the arms of a loving God.

She had told Charlie and Lucy Mae that they were birthed at home, in their little shack on the outskirts of Enid—in hiding, so that no one would ever know they existed—because they were born with blood and sin and corruption upon their shoulders—the devil's spawn—that they were the shameful result of her wicked ways—Satan's constant reminder of her unrighteous life. But one day she had heard Reverend Churchill on the radio. His voice was clear and lucid and Momma had felt the holy light in his words. Hallelulia Jesus! Hallelulia Reverend!!! No more bars, no more fornication! She vowed right then and there to live the rest of her life doing the will of her new God and receiving his eternal forgiveness. He was her non-stop "A" ticket to heaven. Her kids could try to hitchhike their way to pearly gates for all she cared.

Now she did her drinking at home, behind closed doors—a door even her God could not see through—and kept her kids locked up so no one would ever know that she had sinned.

And to protect them from the evils and horrors of the world.

Except for the horrors she visited upon them herself.

CHAPTER FIVE

Meg Stinson unconsciously tugged at her strawish blonde hair. There was a sadness to her smile as she took a courage-bolstering breath, then entered the producer's private office. Trans-Galactica Studios. This place was not glamorous—this was a place that chewed up souls.

It was matinee time.

"Let's get down to business," Sidney Newhouse said with an impatient Cockney accent. "I 'ave a schedule to meet."

He sniffed some white powder into his nostrils, a chubby finger rubbing the residue across his gums as he leaned back in his burgundy-leather desk chair. Like he was the fucking king of the world. But he was far from regal, despite his efforts to lose the Cockney accent that screamed out his humble origins. Even here, in the United States, an accent was a dead giveaway. Ask anyone from the Bronx. Or Jersey. Or the backwoods of Kentucky for that matter.

Hell, the audiences had laughed out loud when a young and handsome Tony Curtis had opened his mouth to speak in *Spartacus*. It was Bernie Schwartz from the Bronx in a toga! The film was a biblical epic complete with New York gangster, accent and all.

That particular casting choice certainly did not fly well with the critics.

But somehow that leading man face and bright baby blues got him through just fine.

Welcome to Hollywood.

Breeding always shows, Meg thought with scorn as her mother's words wedged their way into her mind. Her mother had been right about a few things after all.

This fat man repulsed her.

He always had.

He was nothing but an overstuffed pig with an over-inflated ego.

But he had the power and the connections and that was why she was here. She did not have to like him.

Sidney buzzed his secretary on the intercom and ordered her to hold all calls, then motioned impatiently to Meg.

The bastard.

Meg approached him where he sat behind the teakwood desk. Posters of his movies hung on the paneled walls along with awards and autographed photos of the movie stars that played in them, taunting her. She belonged on that wall too, not the floor, even if it was plushly carpeted!

She eased herself to her knees and unzipped the pants of his expensive suit.

It was time for work.

Meg's mind wandered as she gave Sidney what he expected. Her end of the bargain. At one time she had wanted to be an artist. She was good, too. No one knew better than she how bad choices alter the course of a life. By the time she started figuring things out everything she had ever dreamed seemed out of the question. Priorities had shifted with a thud. Oil and canvas and art supplies cost money. And money was scarce. This cost her nothing—except her pride. So here she was—waiting for the big break that would vindicate her being on her knees in this room.

Blow-jobs for bit parts.

It got her foot in the door.

It paid the bills.

It was a trade-off.

And it was a hell of a lot better than where she had been.

She looked up as Sidney shoved more coke up his pudgy

nose. You Cockney bastard, she thought as she quickly finished the job.

He groaned as his body tensed and jerked, then relaxed.

The business transaction in the office of the Producer's Building at Trans-Galactica Studios was completed. It had taken Meg two minutes to satisfy Sidney Newhouse but she knew the degradation would cling to her much longer. She told herself that she was surviving. She salved her soul by saying that she was buying a better life for her daughter Sabrina and herself. Truth was, she didn't know what else to do.

She was lost.

Sidney wiped off his cock with a silk handkerchief, shoved the limp flesh into his pants and zipped. Meg wished that he would catch his skin in the zipper as he used his other hand to push the intercom button, then ordered his secretary to get Angelo in casting. But he didn't catch it, not today. Instead, he thumbed through a script on his desk as he waited for the call. He flipped through white and pink and yellow and blue pages, each colored sheet representing word changes in the dialogue of an ever-changing story.

The intercom buzzed and Sidney picked up the phone.

"*The Boston Beane's*, Episode 36009," his staccato voice began. "Page twenty-three, scene fourteen. There's a two-line bit about 'alf way down the page. I am sending over Meg Stinson...yeah, she's the one...see that she gets it. Got it?"

At least I don't have to blow Angelo, she thought. He prefers his people with penises, thank God. I got what I came for, she told herself as she wiped the acrid taste of Sidney from her lips. He caught her eye as she was turning to leave, scrawled something on a piece of paper and held it out, waving it impatiently in her direction.

"Party tonight at Tony Savage's. A little celebration over the mini-series deal we just closed. Here's the address." He waved the paper at her again as his other hand wiped the blood and mucous that dripped from what remained of his sinus passages. Hollywood plastic surgeons made a fortune rebuilding the insides of all the industry coke-heads' noses and Sidney was just about due for another visit.

Meg took the piece of paper and smiled sweetly at the producer, masking her contempt for him as she turned toward the door.

She was a good little actress.

The past ten minutes had just proven that, had they not?

There was a well-practiced, quiet dignity to her exit. She was on the other side of the door when the tears came, catching her off guard. A quote by Albert Schweitzer crossed her mind, probably something she had heard in a high school class years ago—"The tragedy of life is what dies inside a man while he lives."

She pushed the thought away and pressed forward.

Meg Stinson avoided eye contact with the secretary in the outer office as she tidied her hair and headed toward Casting.

CHAPTER SIX

Both lawns were mowed, Mr. Owens's and her own, and Sabrina sat at the small flower bed of geraniums at the corner of her lawn—the geraniums she had stolen slip by slip from her neighbor's yard. She loved geraniums. They were tough flowers that survived the snails and neglect and the heat of a Hollywood summer. She liked Mr. Owens's crocuses too, but her mother had warned her against digging up his crocus bulbs. Common old geraniums were one thing, they grew with the ferocity of unwanted weeds in California, but crocuses were another matter altogether. They were nurtured.

Sabrina pushed the hair from her face with a muddy hand. The grit streaked across her perspiring nose. Three freckles marched like fire ants across its bridge, and, but for the color of her hair, looked out of place against her olive skin.

She looked up from where she sat as she heard her mother's car pull into the drive. The old Volkswagen sounded as if it was dying of emphysema. She stood and watched as Meggie bolted from the car and ran to her.

"Sabrina, it's just too great!"

Sabrina followed as her mother flew into the house, catching the door before it closed in her face. She had not seen Meggie so animated in weeks as she related the news of the Tony Savage party to her daughter, then asked Sabrina to help her pick out a dress. It would be an easy task. There were limited wardrobe options.

After sorting through Meg's few good outfits, Sabrina settled on a simple black crepe jumpsuit that would set off her mother's pale skin and soft honey tinted hair. And a simple string of fake pearls. Classic simplicity. Like Grace Kelly or Audrey Hepburn or Dina Merrill.

"I am so sorry sweetie, I know you like it when we can be together, but this could be important. New connections, you know? And it's Tony Savage!"

"Tony Savage? How utterly *hot!* Of course I understand. It's okay, really." She said. "Besides, I already made plans."

"But I cannot understand why I was even invited. I'm a nobody and I'm sure there will be even more big names there than Tony. Why would he ask me?"

"Probably because he knows you're going to be a big name too." Sabrina shifted her weight before adding: "Meggie—I guess I forgot what day it was, but Saturday morning I need a huge favor. All the moms are getting together with the other girls in the Troop. We're going over to Safeway to get rid of the rest of the Girl Scout Cookies. This is our last weekend to get them sold and they'll sell like crazy in front of the store. And besides, I would really like to show you off."

Meg agreed to Saturday morning. Partly out of guilt and obligation, but mostly because she wanted to spend some time with her daughter.

"Meggie, I was over at Mr. Owens's this afternoon. He told me something really weird. Why would someone change their name from Solomon to Owens? I just don't get it."

"Fear, maybe. The poor man has been through a lot. Maybe he's afraid they might find him again."

"Who?"

Meg hesitated. Sabrina was not old enough to know about such things. She tried to chose her words carefully. "Terrible things were done to people during the war. By some miracle he managed to survive, but it's unlikely that he will ever feel safe again. Wars leave deep scars."

"How sad."

Then Meg changed the subject before Sabrina could ask any

more questions.

* * * * * * *

When Sabrina left for the movies she knew that her mother would be the most beautiful woman at the party. Her Meggie was just about the most gorgeous lady in the whole wide world, but she really needed someone to take care of her. She deserved that. Maybe some day a man would come along whom her mother could trust. But until that person comes along, Sabrina thought, I'll just keep taking care of her myself. She felt like a mother to the woman who had become a lost child in her eyes. Looking after her was important to Sabrina and she didn't mind. Not one bit. After all, artistic people needed someone to worry about the mundane things in life.

Meg had more important things to think about than making grocery lists or checking if the old Volkswagen was low on oil. Sabrina found those chores rather fun and it made her feel grown up.

And come Saturday she could show off her beautiful mother to her friends.

She was proud of her Meggie.

CHAPTER SEVEN

Hallelulia brother! Thank you Jesus! the voice bellowed from the radio. Silence and static followed for longer than it should have...then a choir of heavenly angels began to sing Amazing Grace.

The atmosphere in his room was dark and ominous, a lingering sense of doom hovering over the claustrophobic corner that Charlie Blackhawk called his own. He was only ten the first time his mother crawled into his bed. She reeked of whiskey fumes as she invaded his sanctuary and defiled him, robbing him of one of the few things he possessed in his ugly world—his childhood—his innocence. A cigarette dangled from her lips as she straddled him, the long ash falling down and sifting into Charlie's bewildered eyes. He blinked, squeezed them tightly shut. He turned his face from her rancid breath as she exhaled.

"You just be a good boy now and mind your momma," Wilma Blackhawk had said to her Charlie. Charlie knew to mind his momma—NOT minding was a dangerous thing. He had the scars to prove it. This was what mommas and sons were supposed to do, she had told him. What momma and the reverend revealed to him was all the truth he ever had to know. The reading she had taught him was for knowing the bible and the word of God and God said his children must mind their mommas!

He had lain silent in the dark room, surrounded by the aromas of liquor and sour perfume and enveloped by the onrush of new sensations she aroused within him. He was terrified. He *was excited. He dared not speak. She rocked back and forth atop her son, moaning in her drunken pleasure, then stopped abruptly.*

The darkened room cowered in silence.

Charlie cowered in fear.

She grabbed his small penis and squeezed it tightly.

Confusion.

Contradiction.

"You been a bad boy! You brought the devil into our home," she said. "You been really bad Charlie boy and God says I gotta punish my children when they're bad." She slurred the words as she pulled the hot cigarette from her frowning mouth.

* * * * * * *

Clouds the color of licorice whips streaked across the evening sky as Sabrina walked up Gower Street. By the time she crossed Fountain Avenue fat droplets of rain splattered abstractly upon the sidewalk beneath her feet. She quickened her pace, pulled the collar of her ragged sweater to her chin, and turned left onto Hollywood Boulevard. She hated this stretch of the Boulevard. It depressed her. Empty people with emptier eyes wandered the night and unnamed dangers lurked in the shadows and unlit side streets. The bag people and the street musicians were okay, they called her by name, and when she was in no hurry she enjoyed visiting with them. She had made friends here. Old Black Raven, always clutching his beat up clarinet, had taught her about Dizzy Gillespie and Al Hirt and Paul Desmond. Desmond might be white on the outside, he had said, but scratch below the surface and you would find a soul as black as a Louisiana bayou. Gene Krupa played drums like he was possessed. And there was John Coltrane. And Miles Davis. And Eubie Blake. Raven told her wonderful stories about the French Quarter in New Orleans and he had taught her far more than "music appreciation" had ever done at school. Old Black Raven had been a famous jazz musician in the Big Easy—before the heroin had become more important than the music. But he carried the clarinet as if it was an extension of his being and played the notes he could remember and pretended he was still whole.

So many broken people with their broken dreams and broken lives were scattered along the sidewalks. They walked like zombies. Or they stumbled like awkward children. Or they cowered in the alleyways, cringing at the dark unknown.

The Boulevard was a mine field for a young girl, with its pimps and addicts and outright crazies, but Sabrina had learned to sidestep the dangers with the grace of a cat and this place had become her favorite playground.

From out of the corner of her eye she saw The Magic Man sidle up to her. He was a horrid little creature, no bigger than Sammy Davis Jr. on his best day, but he was a destructive force to be reckoned with. Every boulevard denizen knew who The Magic Man was and unless you were looking for him to fill your needs, everyone avoided him. He was the lowest of the low, even by street standards.

"Good evening you pretty little thing," he said, bowing as if he were a gentleman, doffing his purple pimp hat like a weak caricature of Sir Walter Raleigh. But there was nothing noble about him, Sabrina had that figured out the first time she had crossed paths with him.

"Get lost." Sabrina spat the words at the pimp.

"I takes good care of you, sweetness. Be your man. Buys you pretty clothes. I be truthin' you, sweet thing. What you gots is worth mountains of gold on these here streets."

"That's not as much as it's worth to me, slimebag!"

The scenario with the pimp always played out the same, similar to her banter with Mr. Owens but far deadlier in their intent, although he never pushed *too* hard. It wasn't necessary. There were always plenty of desperate victims in his feeding ground—so many that were either dumb enough or willing enough or hungry enough to swallow his pathetic promises.

The Trailways bus turned the corner and pulled into the terminal. Air brakes hissed as it came to a stop. The Magic Man whipped his head around like a weasel picking up a scent. "Next time, baby," he muttered as he slunk away.

"Sure, next time ass-hole," she said.

Sabrina wondered how many runaways would be on the bus tonight. Their hearts would be full of hope. Hope for a better chance at life than the places they had left behind. Dreams were here for the taking, weren't they? Hollywood drew them like a magnet then filled their heads with lies. The city promised them carousels but instead fed them misery and unmarked graves. They were the flotsam and jetsam that fed men like The Magic Man. He would take care of them. He would take such good care of them that they would wonder why they had ever left home. But by then it would be too late. By then their eyes would be dead and the Magic Man would have a new pair of alligator boots.

It was depressing.

Sabrina imagined The Magic Man running to the Trailways, slipping and falling under the wheels as the big bus pulled into the terminal. His pimp hat would fly into the air as the giant tire crushed his skull. She would applaud and Old Black Raven would play at his funeral.

But it wouldn't happen.

Creeps like The Magic Man went on forever.

There was no line in front of the movie theater. Sabrina bought her ticket and went inside. She sat in the darkness waiting for Steven Seagal to come on the screen. Today there was no money for popcorn drowned in the stench of fake butter or a hot dog that had rotated on a grill hours longer than it should have. No loss. She sat there, knees pressed against the back of the seat in front of her, and daydreamed about the father who never was. Chuck Norris's face always appeared when she thought of a father. She had told his story to the kids at school so often that she almost believed it:

Dad had been a real hero. She and her mother still missed him. And her mother knew that there was no man good enough to ever take his place. He had been a Soldier of Fortune and a fighter of noble causes and she still remembered hugging him goodbye for the last time as he left for that fateful mission. He had entered Vietnam via Cambodia to rescue some MIA's in a camp sixty miles north of old Saigon. Only this time the gooks were waiting for him. His name was legend in this part of Asia and they all feared the great American warrior. The cowardly bastards had outnumbered him a hundred to one—but he had managed to kill nineteen of the slant-eyes before they finally got him. They tied him up and tortured him for hours. Her father had died a heroes death out there in the humid, overgrown jungle. But even dead the gooks were afraid of him, so they had whacked him to bloody little pieces with their machetes—just to be sure—and scattered pieces of him along a five mile radius of the spot where he had died. He had no grave but he would never be forgotten. Sabrina's father was a legend—

and sometimes it was nearly real.

The curtain opened, exposing the screen. Sabrina counted the gashes where empty popcorn boxes had been hurled against the screen. To the lower left, some cola had left a long streak of drying drool where a cup had been tossed by some disrespectful punk. The theater lights slowly dimmed until the room was enveloped by darkness. The projector started up with a tsch, tsch sound, lighting up the screen. The scars hardly showed once the previews started, and once the movie began to play she didn't notice them at all.

The transformation to her magical world had begun.

There was a faint aroma of sour vomit in the theater—the tinkling sound of some rummy's empty bottle as it rolled forward on the slanted floor. The all-night theater was a dark place that didn't give up her secrets—a place where horny teen-agers or unfaithful spouses could make out, unseen. It was a cheap night's lodging for the homeless hordes when the flop-houses and shelters were full and the cushioned seats provided comfortable barstools for the crowd that drank their poison from brown paper bags. It was a place for dirty men to do nasty things alone, blanketed in the murky shadows.

For Meg Stinson it was a place to become....

Sylvester Stallone pushing his way to the top with sweat and muscle—

Chuck Norris winning out with wits and martial arts—

Charles Bronson righting the injustices of the world through the barrel of a gun—

Even Arnold Schwartz-its, with his goofy accent, outsmarting some villain or another, saving not only his own ass but that of the free world in one fell swoop.

This was Sabrina's favorite place—no contest.

CHAPTER EIGHT

It was dusk as Meg Stinson turned the old Volkswagen off of Laurel Canyon and headed up toward Mount Olympus. The development was one step down from the stately Mediterranean mansions of the old Hollywood or Beverly Hills, devoid of the latter's faded glamour with its aged Spanish tile roofs and grand staircases and heart-shaped swimming pools. It was a newer place for even newer faces. Million dollar houses high atop the hills pretending at being classical Greek. Even the street names reflected Greek gods. It was Hollywood pretension at its pathetic norm, but an envious address nonetheless. Meg wanted to park farther down the hill to hide her German beater but could find no space to park so she swallowed her pride and pulled up in front of the estate. A parking attendant in a white jacket opened the car door for her and took the keys. He had a nice face and looked just like a thousand other unemployed actors who worked odd jobs waiting for the big break that never came. They parked cars, waited tables, drove taxis, turned tricks and eventually faded away. Or went back to Kansas or wherever they came from and settled for a life of selling insurance and breeding brats in the suburbs.

Dreams died in this town by the millions. But on rare occasion one would be realized. That was the carrot dangling before them, just beyond reach. It was the lottery everybody banked on, the ticket they scrambled to buy regardless of the price.

The first hour or so Meg tried her hand at *working the room,* as they like to say. Unsuccessfully. Assertiveness was *not* her strong suit, so her attempts at idle conversation fell flat. She just didn't register with them and their blank stares and rude indifference let her know it. Meg wished she had never come. She didn't know anyone and wondered why she had even been invited. She certainly didn't feel as if she fit in—a total nobody surrounded by somebodies. It was awkward and uncomfortable. Her daughter Sabrina always said how proud she was of her—but even her biggest fan would surely be embarrassed by tonight's flop.

The party was in full swing, a Who's Who of producers, directors, an Academy Award winning composer, actresses and actors from both television and features. Today's shining stars, tomorrow's has-beens. A cluster of sound-alike singers chatted away as if unaware they were headed for the graveyard of *no-longer-relevant*—once a tv essential, they were headed for the dust bin thanks to *Miami Vice*. They could be The Pointer Sisters, John Fogerty, Sinatra—anyone you needed them to be, at a fraction of the cost. The original artists who would have been real budget busters. The illusion was all that mattered and this town banked on illusion. But Michael Mann had set the standard into the stratosphere with his Jan Hammer soundtrack and original recordings such as Phil Collins's *In the Air Tonight*. The music was having as much impact as the stars and scripts. Audiences ate it up and budgets be damned. Thanks to Mann, a commodity Universal Studios was thrilled to have, ten thousand here and twenty grand there for sixty seconds of music was fast becoming the new television standard. And the sound-alikes? They were speeding down the fast track to obsolescence quicker than Sonny Crockett's fake 1972 Ferrari Daytona Spider and sinking faster than his Endeavor 42 sailboat in a Miami hurricane. But even they were more "in" than Meg.

Gideon Stark from the Hollywood Reporter was there talking to the owner of this week's trendy Beverly Hills bistro. By next week the in-crowd would discover another place, an even trendier place, to show themselves off. Everything in this town was fickle, elusive and ever-changing. The players, with the attention spans of little children, dropped one toy and picked up another, newer one whenever it caught their eye. Appearances were everything. As was being seen in the right places. Restaurants flourished, then went belly-up with their every whim. They lined up in front of exclusive nightspots, being motioned inside because of who they were while others were rudely dismissed and denied entry. A glamorous clientele made a place. And destroyed it just as swiftly. The transition from *in* to *so yesterday* could be brutally swift, the watering holes changing faster than the latest fads and fashions.

Three studio lawyers sipped cocktails and scanned the room for starlets in hopes of getting a quick lay before heading back to Encino and their waiting wives. The days of a handshake as a contract were as gone as the *Baby Jane's* with their ringlets, rouge and rosebud lips. Now the studios had entire legal departments packed with attorneys who spent their days dreaming up complex contracts filled with enough legalese and loopholes that none but the most jaded and savvy could figure out that the odds were always stacked in favor of the house. The business had become as clever as a Las Vegas casino and as crooked as Washington D.C. As a rule, there was far more creativity in the bookkeeping than there was on the screen.

Alcohol and drugs flowed freely but Meg Stinson didn't help herself to the drugs, instead motioning to the bartender to refill her champagne glass for the fifth time. She was getting buzzed. She walked through the wall of people to a life-size porcelain Buddha, leaned against its big belly and observed her surroundings.

A smallish man worked the room on his way toward her. In his one hand he held a drink while his other hand was clenched into an awkward fist at his side. He walked as if his feet were on rollers, swaying slightly from side to side as he approached. He was young, his appearance Chaplinesque. Chocolate eyes reflected uneasiness and avoided direct contact.

He was wound tighter than an old maid's underpants.

"I should know you," he said. "I'm sorry. Jason Mittleman.

I'm with The William Morris Agency. You are beyond beautiful—it just seems I should recognize you from something... what are you working on?"

"A hangover," said Meg.

"Not to offend," he stammered. "It's just—it's just that you have that wonderful, burned-out Monroe quality. That combo of brazen sexuality and helplessness." He tilted his head to the side as he searched for the right words. "That vulnerability—it melts men's hearts and makes the lesbos want to devour you. It makes people want to ravage you and protect you at the same time."

"Just go away," Meg said.

"But I just can't take my eyes off you. God, I'm melting...I'm melting!" Jason smiled, wiped his brow with an exaggerated gesture.

"Get lost."

"I...."

"Leave me alone." With the taste of Sidney Newhouse fresh on her tongue, Meg was in no mood for fending off some simpering cocker spaniel with Dirk Bogard eyes and a lame come-on.

"There's a goldmine in your face—and your body. Soft and white, like you would rather be screwing than doing aerobics. Jeez, men are tired of humping anorexic females with plastic tits."

Meg bristled. "Looks can be deceiving. I don't believe in anything that promotes perspiration—including sex—and certainly not with you."

Meg averted his gaze, focusing on the room. The scene before her looked like a Hieronymus Bosch painting, the atmosphere grotesque. Three bodies made love in a koi pond. People intertwined on couches while others snorted coke. The room full of laughter and small talk drowned out Etta James's smoldering voice that emanated from the stereo speakers. AT LAST, she was singing, the perfect song. So wrong, Meg thought, a voice like that deserves silent worship. Tony Savage, with his deceptive boy-next-door good looks, was free-basing at the coffee table while a handful of people surrounded him in silent admiration and others stood around in polite conversation as if oblivious to their surroundings. For a split second Tony looked up and made eye contact with her, a slight smile on his sexy mouth, a nearly indistinguishable wink from his smoldering eyes. Meg didn't miss much, but in her alcoholic blur she had not noticed Sidney Newhouse as he approached her. The producer ignored Jason as he spoke.

"Tony wants to see you—now," he said.

Meg gasped.

"Just what are you saying, Sidney?"

"I'm saying he wants a sample. You oughtta be flattered."

She stiffened.

"He's waiting!" Sidney shouted.

Heads turned in their direction.

Well, no one noticed me before, Meg thought, but they sure as hell can see me now!

She recoiled as everyone's gaze focused on the two of them. She wanted to crawl inside herself and silently die there. What she did behind closed doors was between Sidney and herself and the rest of the world was none the wiser. Now she felt as if he had stripped her naked in front the entire room.

It had become evident why she was invited.

Jason Mittleman just stood there silently watching the script unfold before him.

Working up her courage, she said: "Are you pimping now Sidney? Tell Tony to take a flying fuck. Take one yourself while you're at it. I'm not interested." She turned and walked toward the front door, determined to save herself from further humiliation. The bastard had just as much as called her a whore. Her only consolation was that nobody there even knew who the hell she was. And until this minute could have cared less.

She heard Sidney's voice bellowing from across the room. "You're going to regret this, you stupid cunt."

A hush fell over the entire house. Nobody wanted to miss

this scene.

"Do you think you were asked here for bloody damn window dressing? Or because you're *important*? You're nothing but a nameless bit player best left on the cutting room floor." He was getting visibly flustered as he continued his rant. "You belong in some Soho knocking shop," he said, unaware that his audience was likely unfamiliar with his oh so British insult. "You are *nobody*," he said. "You should be grateful that a *somebody* even wants to touch that overworked quim of yours."

The crowd watched in silence as Meg turned to face the fat man.

"Fuck you and the big white horse you rode in on, you Limey pig," she said, then turned and exited.

What had started as an exciting night full of promise had swiftly crumbled to ruin.

The chill night air caused her to shiver as she waited for the attendant to bring her car. The sound of footfalls caused her to turn, primed for another altercation. It was Jason Mittleman.

"God, I don't know if you're the biggest fool in town...."

"I know. I'm dead here."

"...or the smartest or what but you should have heard the buzz when you walked out! Who the hell was that, they said—and they were laughing at *him*. What an exit! Christ, I wish I had it on tape. I would use it for your screen test."

"I know I blew it, but...."

"Every other woman in the room would have fucked Tony Savage at the drop of a hat. Every one but you! That was pretty damn impressive. Hey, I passed out five business cards on my way out—told them I represent you."

"How could you do that? He has the power to destroy me in this shit town."

"Are you kidding? You've got balls lady and now half the town knows it—people just as important as Newhouse. Hell, we'll just keep your interviews away from Trans-Galactica for awhile. It's not the only studio in town," he said, handing her his card. "So, how about it?"

Meg's head buzzed from all the confusion and too much champagne. She got in her car. It sputtered and choked as she revved up the engine.

"A Ferrari!" she heard Jason yell as she drove away. "You'll be driving a fucking Ferrari!"

CHAPTER NINE

Charlie Blackhawk's Nova sped along Highway 247. It was his favorite indirect route to the mountains. Charlie liked traveling the back roads. He stomped on the gas pedal. The car lurched, immediately picking up more speed.

It knew how to mind Charlie.

He felt as if he could see forever along this flat expanse of scrub country. No fucking cops as far as the eye could see. No trouble here.

Just open space, empty and free.

Static belched from the speakers as a country station drifted in and out. But he didn't notice. He was singing his own song as the speedometer needle rose.

"Momma's don't let you're...."

Mommas. Mommas were bad! His mind raced back in time, eyes twitching to the beat of the speakers. Mommas. *Mommas.* The Nova had slowed to forty as Charlie Blackhawk wandered in and out of his mind's darkest places. His squeezed his eyes tightly shut, then opened them wide as he regained his bearings. His muscles were taut, skin drawn white against his knuckles as his hands choked the steering wheel and his foot pressed hard on the accelerator. He stared ahead and felt as if he were flying as the car picked up speed. The Nova ate up the ribbon of deserted highway faster than an anteater sucking up insects.

Up ahead, he spotted a hitchhiker. What was he doing in the middle of nowhere, standing there with his thumb out and a smile on his face? Nobody was ever on this road. That was why he liked it. Charlie debated speeding up even more and hitting the guy head on, propelling him airborne and into the ditch. That would be a kick. Just to see the expression on his face as he flew bug-eyed over the windshield. Thud! Splat! But curiosity—and opportunity—got the best of Charlie, so he slowed down and pulled over. He rolled down the passenger side window and gave his best howdy-do smile as the skinny-ass kid trotted up to his car wearing a grin as big as Texas.

"Hey, thanks mister."

"Where you headed, son?" Charlie asked.

"All the way up to Oregon."

"I'm not going that far, but I can take you a ways in the right direction if you like. Hop in."

The kid, no more than twenty at best, slid into the seat next to Charlie. His luggage consisted of a brown grocery bag and he smelled as if his last shower was weeks behind him. His naive grin exposed a rotten front tooth. He fished in the paper bag, retrieved a cigarette and lit it.

A Camel.

"Best damn smoke on the planet," said Charlie, lighting his own. "How come you're not traveling the main route? It's gonna take a long time this way."

"People are pretty cautious about picking up hitchhikers, so whenever I get an offer I just take it. Been doing a lot of zigzagging along the way, but I keep heading north for the most part. It's been one cool adventure, dude," he said. "Hey, I really appreciate your picking me up. I just hope that when I get there the job is still waiting."

Charlie small-talked, all nice and warm and friendly, as he sized up the kid. This was going to be easy as apple pie and twice as tasty.

"What's the job?" Charlie asked, not really giving a dead rats ass.

The kid hesitated, then shrugged. He felt he was street wise enough to read people and the driver seemed harmless—even friendly. He didn't look like the kind who would judge him, much less turn him in or kick him back to the side of the road.

"Uh, a guy back in L.A. turned me on to it, man. There's these dudes with a going business up there—in the national forest. Deep in the forest, if you get what I mean. They're just looking for a few guys to guard the crops and keep people away, y'know? Sounds like easy money to me."

"What kind of crops?" Charlie asked.

"The kind that keep you happy and chilled out, man."

"You mean marijuana? Isn't that illegal?" Charlie asked, then laughed at his attempt at moral indignation.

"Hey, if it weren't for lumber and pot, Oregon'd have no economy at all. So's they pretty much look the other way up there. It ain't nuthin' like down here, man. Pretty cool, huh? Down here you're always looking over your shoulder and the man is always on your ass waiting to bust you. Seems a waste of pig power when there's real crooks to pick on. Shit, it oughta be legal, man—a little pot never hurt anybody."

Except for numbing his fucking dumb brain, Charlie thought as he reached in the back for a warm beer and handed it to the kid. The kid popped it open and guzzled like a parched Bedouin who had finally reached an oasis in some endless desert. It was warm, sure, but it was damn good. They drank and talked and smoked their way along another five miles of road, and with each passing mile the kid liked this stranger more. Too bad this guy wasn't going the whole distance. He was kinda fun.

And the free beer was a welcome bonus that eased the hunger pains.

Best ride he'd had all day. Hell, best ride he'd had the whole damn trip.

"You're a cool guy, man, thanks. Beer is a damn good breakfast."

"Breakfast of champions," Charlie said. "You look kinda hungry," he said, reaching in the back again and pulling out a bag of pork rinds. "Have some of these. It's not much, but they are pretty filling. All that air helps fill the gullet."

The kid downed them faster than Charlie could recite a dirty limerick, then upended the bag and shook the crumbs into his mouth, crumpled the bag and tossed it to the floor. "Thanks man, that was my first meal in two days," he belched. "You were so cool to pick me up. Most people just drive on by."

"When I was younger I spent plenty of time on the road myself. I remember what it was like, hunger and all, so I am always more than happy to help a fellow traveler."

"Thanks again, man. You must have some awesome karma going."

For the next few minutes they rode in silence, and then Charlie saw the perfect spot.

"I don't know about you kid, but I have to piss like a race-horse."

"Yeah, me too. But I sure wish that beer had managed to hang around a little longer."

Charlie had been more than generous with the little twerp, more than he had to be for sure, but the kid was begging for more of his generosity. Unappreciative little shit, he thought.

"I'll give you another one when we get back to the car," said Charlie.

He pulled the car off the road and into a small copse of trees and scrub. He turned off the key. The two of them got out of the car and walked into the brush and stood tall and still as they prepared to relieve their bladders. Like some sweet old family photo of a father and son outing. As soon as the kid got unzipped Charlie was on him, grabbing him by the throat.

"Wha..." was all the kid could say before the pressure of Charlie's hands around his neck cut off his words. He lowered the kid to the ground, never easing up on his grip. The kid's eyes bugged and he pissed his pants—and probably shit himself, too—as Charlie throttled the life out of him. He stared into the kid's eyes as they filled with little red pinpoints and the expression went milky and blank. It was his easiest kill in a long time, no challenge at all, which took half the fun out of it.

He felt cheated.

But it had perked up his morning and took the monotony out

of an otherwise boring drive.

So the kid had served a positive purpose after all. The kid had been right about one thing, Charlie was certainly having awesome good karma today.

He grabbed the kid's bony ankles and dragged his body under a nearby tree, then covered it with dry brush. Nobody'd ever miss him, Charlie told himself—just one more pothead who'd hit the open road and never looked back. His momma was probably glad to be rid of him. Before anyone stumbled across the body, if by some miracle they ever did, the kid's skin would be leathered up like some old Egyptian mummy.

"Amen, hallelulia!"

He walked back to the Nova. Sitting behind the steering wheel he reached over to the floor on the passenger side and picked up the kid's paper bag, fishing through it for his booty. He pulled out a small bag of weed and tossed it out the window. He didn't like pot. It smelled bad. And it could get a person in trouble. Not much else there. He counted out thirty-seven bucks in wrinkled bills and shoved them into his pocket, then tossed the kid's three packs of Camels onto the passenger seat. He guessed it was better than nothing.

And it had been fun.

Hadn't the kid's mother ever told him hitchhiking could be dangerous? Did she really even give a fuck? He doubted it.

Charlie turned on the engine and sped down the road. The outline of distant mountains came into focus, reminding him of his destination. Muscles relaxed as he reached across the seat for a pack of smokes.

CHAPTER TEN

On Friday Sabrina Stinson awoke with a start. The strange events of the previous night reassembled themselves quickly, taking form in her mind. Through the early morning dimness she watched her mother in deep slumber at her side. Meg had still been at the party when it happened, her side of the bed empty.

Sabrina had been lying in bed, in that twilight state between wakefulness and sleep. As her mind drifted, she became aware of an odd sensation—like an electrical current. She felt the pulsation surround her until it felt more real than the body which lay on the sheets. She sensed herself ascending. Upon opening her eyes she was surprised to be looking down at her own form on the bed.

It was scary.

A shimmering silver cord rose from her body and stretched to where she hovered near the ceiling. A magical window had opened in her mind revealing vibrant colors and perceptions. She looked down at her body and wondered if she was dying— if this was what it felt like to be lifted to heaven. If God was lifting her she felt awe rather than fear. She floated across the ceiling like a phantasm—like she imagined it felt to jump from a plane and drift in the clouds.

A barely audible noise jarred her. She felt a swirling rush, faster than light, and descended in ever contracting circles, reentering her form with a thud. The weight of her body felt unpleasant.

She opened her eyes.

This had been no dream.

* * * * * * *

North of Los Angeles, in the master-planned community of Hidden Meadows, lack of sleep had left Amy Hamill exhausted and hungry.

She pushed the horrifying memory of another bad dream from her mind. Her mother was in the dream. When she asked her why she wasn't tall and pretty too, all her mother had said was: "You know you're adopted."

And then the bad man had appeared.

Amy grabbed a banana from the kitchen counter, picked up her school books, then slammed the front door behind her, glad that this was Friday. Weekends never felt as lonely as the classroom. No one, especially not her father, knew what courage it took to face the daily taunting and teasing. But today was Friday.

Amy quickened her step as she spotted Freddy at the corner. He was the only kid who had gone out of his way to befriend her. He was an outcast too. Fat Freddy the Freak—Porky the Computer Nerd. They made quite a pair as they quietly joined forces. They walked down the sidewalk, tall Freddy waddling along as the little pixie doubled her pace to keep up with him.

"I don't want to do it," Amy said. "Why does Miss Walker make us do oral reports anyway?"

"You can't afford being knocked down a grade, so do it and get it over with," he puffed. "Just keep your eyes on me when you're talking."

* * * * * * *

Amy's legs felt like Jell-O® as she stood at the front of the room. The papers quivered as she held them. She took a deep breath and focused her gaze on Freddy. He sat in the last seat of the third row and signaled encouragement.

Then it happened.

A queer dizziness blind-sided her. The segues were becoming more frequent and as she gasped for air she was aware that they were becoming harder to control. A deep breath did not help. Counting to ten didn't help either. Her tiny hands flailed through the air in an effort to retain her balance but there was nothing for her to grab hold of. Darkness swirled in pulsating circles before her eyes. She felt her knees give way and tried to focus on Freddy's face but it melted in a blur. She closed her eyes—tried to regain her bearings. The loud buzzing in her ears fogged her consciousness. Her papers fell as she held her hands to her ears and shut her eyes tightly.

Slowly, she regained awareness of her surroundings.

She was sitting on the floor.

The other children were tittering but her friend Freddy was kneeling at her side. All she wanted to do was to crawl under a desk and hide. Freddy stood and held his hands out to Amy, helping her to stand as she tried to muster her composure. As she looked at him for reassurance he whispered in her ear, "You called Miss Walker a nasty name."

Tears welled in Amy's eyes for she remembered nothing beyond the dizziness. Uncontrollable, she thought, attempting to swallow the fear that lumped like a ball of Play-doh in her throat.

"I'm sorry Miss Walker. Please, I can continue now."

Amy bent over and picked up the papers that were strewn across the floor. Her hands trembled as she tried to block the laughter.

"You're going straight to the principal's office," the teacher said. "Freddy, return to your seat!"

"Please, no," Amy whimpered. "Please...."

CHAPTER ELEVEN

In a run-down house on a run-down street in Hollywood, the sun beat defiantly through the torn sheet nailed over the bedroom window. Motes of dust wafted through the broken pane, dancing and drifting in slivers of interloping sunlight. Meg Stinson groaned as she pulled herself from the bed, her puffy eyelids wrapped in agony and last night's thick charcoal eyeliner. She had a full-blown hangover—even her eyelashes hurt. Her waking thoughts had been of family, thoughts that gnawed like rats on electrical wire as she walked down the hallway and into the kitchen.

She had run away years ago. After all, teenagers had all the answers. She had managed to screw things up big time and that fact was not an easy thing to admit. She had lost all confidence in her own judgment and in herself. Her mother had become a faceless voice the past few months since she had started phoning her. It was time to start healing old wounds. The conversations were awkward and uncomfortable at first. There was so much that had to be left unsaid. So much that was unnecessary for her mother to know. Her lost runaway daughter had finally resurfaced and that was enough. She was alive instead of dead in a ditch somewhere. Meg had finally told her about Sabrina but was yet to tell Sabrina about her grandmother, except for the fact that one existed out there somewhere. The woman's blood was blue and never clashed with the decor. Meg wondered how she had managed to fall so far from the illustrious family tree. But fall she had, with a thud.

"Jeez kid, you've really got your dick in the dirt this morning," Betty said. "How's about some coffee to bring you back to the world of the living?"

Meg took the mug from her friend. Betty topped the scales at three-hundred pounds and could laugh at anything. Meg wished she could be more like her. Meg was a Russian drama, while her friend was a comedy of the absurd. She and Sabrina were Meg's stability. Someone who had started out as a roommate to help defray expenses had quickly become their dearest friend.

"You should learn to sleep instead of partying so hard,' said Betty. "You look like hell."

"This time might have been worth it—or it might have destroyed everything," Meg said with a shrug. She related the previous night's events to her friend. "And I've got an agent. With The William Morris Agency."

"Wow. But William Morris? Isn't that the place where agents and actors disappear never to be heard from again?"

"Yeah, it's too big for sure, but it definitely has a reputation to match it's size."

Betty had switched from coffee to hot chocolate. As she prodded Meg for all the details her spoon would capture a marshmallow, push it below the surface of steaming liquid, then watch as it bobbed to the surface. One by one she rescued them and sucked them into her mouth. Meg unconsciously doodled on a scratch pad as they spoke, a talent Betty admired, always taking the small pictures and displaying them on the fridge. "You draw beautifully," she said. "God would not have given you such a wonderful talent unless he wanted you to use it."

Ignoring her, Meg said, "I feel guilty I wasn't up for Sabrina this morning."

"I wouldn't worry. She's one self-sufficient kid. She had her lunch packed and was out the door before I even had the coffee made. You've got one hell of a kid there, lady."

Meg knew Sabrina was special. She was pretty and straight A smart—too smart to make her mother's mistakes. "But I worry—for a couple of reasons. She's so hot tempered and she still has invisible playmates like a three-year-old. I know that I'm to blame. I haven't given her much of a life and there is no sense of family...of continuity...of stability." There had been so many mistakes best left unspoken. She told Betty how she had always felt like an outcast, how her mother had clung to her heritage as if it were a living, breathing thing that pulled her from her own generation—her living family. Since childhood Meg felt unable to measure up to the old tintypes in the antique velvet album. She resented the yellowed images and wished they could come to life so that her mother could see they weren't perfect—that she could see that even *they* had flaws. Her mother was the perfectionist, cold and aristocratic. She nurtured the old photos as if they were rare orchids.

Connecticut had been especially beautiful in the fall of that long-lost year. The trees were draped in autumn calico, their fallen leaves dancing like Cyd Charisse in a magical Brigadoon as they drifted to the sidewalks and blanketed the earth.

But Meg had argued with her mother that morning.

"You're unfocused and lazy, Mary Margaret," her mother had said. "And you are capable of far better grades."

Meg played hooky that day and went to the Foster's Freeze instead. Junior Barnes sat in the adjacent booth, a stranger passing through. They struck up a conversation. He was so super-cool, a real grown up with his own car. A rebel who told her she could come along with him to the west coast. Who could resist that?

No one noticed as Meg climbed into the blue van that waited in the shadow of the old elm tree. Her mother would have said he was unsavory, the type that hangs out at laundromats and bus stops and trailer parks—hell, that was reason enough to team up right there! That'd show her.

Meg had helped map out their route to California (what a team). They dined on burgers and beer and fries and by ten-thirty-five p.m. she had lost her virginity. That night, at a small motel, physical violence replaced the gothic romance of her adolescent fantasy. He had thrust into her with the sensitivity and speed of a jackhammer. (You're mine now.) When she screamed his fist silenced her as his weapon drove deep inside her.

You can't go home.

When they reached the coast he told her it was time to earn her keep. That was the night he brought home the first stranger. She learned to move as a shadow and she learned to survive.

You can't go home again, right Thomas Wolfe?

Meg wondered if the girl with autumn leaves dancing in her heart could ever come alive again, or if she had really died in that motel room after all.

"Such a sad, sad face." Betty's voice snapped her back.

"Life's a bitch," said Meg.

"Yeah, like when you're in your twenties you are gonna save the world but when you hit thirty you realize you can't change a fucking thing. By the time you're forty all you want to save is your own ass—or have it tucked."

They laughed.

"When I see her again—my mother—I don't want to be judged."

"Ain't one of us hasn't been a disappointment to our parents. My old man had wanted a son, he made no bones about that, so I spent half my life seeking his approval. I fished and hunted and wore Levi's and flannel shirts. I played ball with him. I watched football and wrestling instead of playing with dolls. I tried to be his perfect son. Shit, I did everything I could this side of growing a dick. Never regret and never apologize. Be you, not what you think other people want you to be." She told Meg she had figured out that seed of eternal wisdom on the day she had put on her sexiest negligee, downed thirty-five Valium with a fifth of Irish and flopped around in her own puke for two days. Between bouts of vomiting and hallucinations, she waited for Prince Charming to appear and rescue her, but he had forgotten to come. It was one hell of a wake up call, but it had done the trick. She owned her own life from that day forward.

"Time to lighten up," Betty laughed. "Time to eat!"

Betty shoved a piece of Sara Lee® cheesecake into her mouth.

"Damn that's good shit. I know food is my drug of choice but I have really got to diet."

"You're a perfect work of art just as you are."

"A perfect Rubens, right? Rubenesque is just a complimentary way of saying grossly obese. That look has been out of fashion for centuries. C'mon Meg, you know I'm killing myself with this stuff,' she said, putting another spoonful of cheesecake into her mouth and exhaling a soft purr. "It's glorious suicide by food. Oh, what the hell, I'm killing myself with the L.A. smog and the cigarettes anyway. I guess it's all just a game of choose your poison. And who in their right mind would turn down a poison that tastes so damn fucking good? But tomorrow...yes, tomorrow...."

"You could have your mouth wired shut," Meg laughed.

"You know me better than that. If they wired my mouth shut I would just figure out how to eat my food vaginally."

CHAPTER TWELVE

Charlie Blackhawk's Nova wound its way up the Rim of the World Highway and pulled up in front of the General Store. He turned off the ignition, got out of the car and slammed the door. He entered the store and walked to the Post Office window located in the rear. The place smelled like a blend of musty attic mixed with pine cleaner and pipe tobacco. The floor was of worn, wooden planks and looked like it had been lying there for the best part of forever. Charlie liked this place.

It felt good to be back at Pine Lake.

He didn't like much in this world, but he liked the sound of dead pine needles as they snapped beneath his boots like brittle bones and their tart aroma when he took a deep breath of mountain air. There was a peacefulness here than he found nowhere else. A solitude. A place where he could come and go unobserved. Charlie had the advantage of being easy on the eyes. He was no Robert Redford but he was no Dustin Hoffman either. He was a chameleon. He was a charmer when it suited his purposes. Just a slightly above average face that would leave no deep impression one way or the other. It made keeping a low profile easy. He saw himself as looking as harmless as anyone else and he felt he could blend into a crowd unnoticed. He was the fucking Invisible Man and he liked it that way.

"Would you check the General Delivery box for Charles Blackhawk, darlin'?" he said to the young woman behind the counter. Jan Smith looked at Charlie, her darkly painted eyes peering at him through layers of mascara right out of the sixties although she could not have been more than twenty. Her raven hair was spiked above her ears. Tiny, braless breasts pointing through her t-shirt provided the only hint as to her gender. PARTY WITH SPUDS, her shirt proclaimed. She winked at Charlie, then turned to the row of boxes behind her.

Slut! Shameless hussy! Charlie's mother whispered the words into his brain. Tramp, disease-ridden whore!

Jan looked at his tanned face and intense gray eyes. There was something familiar about those eyes that looked at you and through you at the same time. She could smell the danger and she liked the aroma. She ruffled through the mail, then handed it to him, ever so slowly—even sensually. If one could manage to hand over the mail sensually she certainly knew how to deliver!

Charlie's eyes broke away from the young woman's gaze and glanced around the store. A kid stood at the register with a fistful of licorice. "Looks like you got a customer," he said as he turned from the devil's temptation and headed for the food aisles. Been too abrupt, he thought. He did not want to draw attention to himself. He just wanted to be alone. But the child-like breasts on the bitch aroused him. Why would she do that when he was trying so hard to behave? To be invisible.

No Charlie, he reminded himself, you don't shit too close to where you eat.

He picked up what he needed and unloaded the groceries at the register. Cheese, toilet paper, crackers, crunchy peanut butter, a box of macaroni and cheese, beer, a pack of batteries.

And kerosene.

The damned bastards had probably disconnected everything by now. Never mind that their decision would have been due to his lack of payment. Charlie saw that as beside the point. Every negative result that came from one of his actions was seen as someone else's fault—someone else to blame for his own failings. Electricity! It seemed as if everything had to be plugged into something these days.

Damn, but he'd like to plug something into that tight little pussy at the counter.

Stop it, Charlie, he told himself. Just get what you need and get the hell out of here.

"Can I ring this stuff up for you...Charles?" Jan said. "Gee, it don't look like you're planning on being around long. Too bad," she winked.

She was prying. Nosy. He did not like that. Not one bit.

"I almost forgot—a carton of Camel Filters. And a box of those night crawlers."

"You live near the lake?

There she goes again.

"More or less."

"You know it's not fishing season yet."

Then why is she selling bait? He was tempted to say it, but didn't. Stop it, just fucking stop it, he thought giving her a look that shut her up.

The nosy little bitch packed up his two bags of supplies and handed them to him. He could not see her eyeing his backside as he turned to leave. His cold look had not discouraged her one bit. It had turned her on. She liked a challenge almost as much as she liked the smell of danger. Jan watched as he loaded his groceries into an old Chevy Nova. The license plate read HAWK—the bumper sticker: MEAN AS A RED-ASSED SPIDER.

She hoped he would be running out of groceries real soon—and that he had a big appetite.

Her gaze followed him as his car turned up at the Wagon Wheel and onto the unpaved road that wound back into the mountains until he was out of sight.

* * * * * * *

Tall pines hovered overhead like treacherous monsters as Charlie's Nova wound its way home. Potholes were filled with mud and water from recent rains, and snow, no longer winter white, lay in grimy patches along the sides of the road.

He liked the seclusion. No little boys with fishing poles

in March. Most of the cabins were empty. Too late for skiers and too early for fishing and camping. This was the solitude he relished. Even in summer Pine Lake only got the overload. Everyone headed for Big Bear or Lake Arrowhead where there was activity and action and plenty of people, leaving this little corner of the San Bernardino Mountains undisturbed. That was its appeal—why he had bought a cabin here in the first place. It was the only thing in life that waited for him. Wherever he wandered the cabin waited for him, like an obedient wife who never asked awkward questions.

Like...where have you been, Charlie...what have you been up to?

After passing a few empty cabins, Charlie reached the familiar fork in the road. The weathered wood sign pointed down to the right and read TO LAKE. He took the narrow road that climbed up to his left. It was barely wide enough for one car, much less a dinosaur Chevy. He was certain that it was meant to be merely a footpath as he gunned the Nova up the steep incline. The engine churned and smoked, the tires spun and gravel spit into the air until he pulled it over and turned off the key. The cabin roof peeked out from over the ridge. He was close enough to make the ascent on foot. No sense chancing problems like when he had scraped the oil pan across some fucking boulder two seasons back.

Charlie was in no mood for problems.

He pocketed the keys, threw the mail into a grocery bag and hiked up the hill. The beer was getting warm and he was thirsty.

It felt good to be home.

As soon as the key slid into the lock Charlie Blackhawk knew that something was wrong. It didn't feel as if it were locked. He picked up his bags, pushing the door open with his shoulder. Charlie had the instincts of a predator, ever aware of the faintest scent on the wind. Even before his eyes adjusted to the darkness the reek of intrusion assaulted him.

"Fucking hippie misfits," he said.

He walked across the room and into the kitchen, putting his

bags down on the kitchen table. Crusted dishes lay in the sink, crawling with ants. He smashed a line of them with his fist, then turned on the hot water spigot to scald them. It sputtered and belched air. No hot water. His frustration escalated. He checked the inside of the cupboard and let out a yelp.

"Bastards!" he yelled, spinning in circles. "You fucking creeps took all three boxes of my Peanut Butter Patties Girl Scout Cookies! Those were mine!"

He walked back to the main room, assessing the damage. The stone fireplace was heaped with trash and the sofa bed was opened. Three empty bottles of Jack Daniels lay on the bare mattress. But nothing else appeared to be disturbed. How the hell did they get in? Had he left the place unlocked? Shit. Damn. If he had left it locked they would just have broken a window. They did things like that. They broke into places. They used them and trashed them. They had no respect for anyone or anything. But it didn't look as though they had destroyed or stolen anything—except for his cookies—and that alone was beyond forgiveness. He thought how good it would feel to find them and wring their skinny little necks until he felt the verte-brae pop. Like that stupid kid on the road. That greedy kid who smoked dope and begged rides from strangers.

Someone had invaded his space.

Soiled his sanctuary.

Who's been sleeping in my bed? Said Papa Bear.

Charlie was pissed.

He opened a beer and pried open a can of Hash with a hand-opener, setting them on the dresser next to the sofa bed. He lit a match to the trash in the fireplace, then sat down on the mattress and imagined a naked teenage girl screwing some pimply-faced geek on his bed. He watched the flames as he ate. He sat and watched the fire as if it were some TV set receiving its signal straight from the bowels of hell. It spoke to him. He watched until twilight fell and the flames had turned to smol-dering embers.

Charlie's eyes fixated on the Girl Scout calendar nailed onto the wall. It was turned to October 1974. The page was yellowed with age and dotted with fly crap. He smiled and the little girl in the photograph smiled back. She stood in her green uniform surrounded by a fall landscape painted the colors of her hair. The dim light from the fireplace danced across her face and Charlie knew that she was smiling just for him.

God, how he loved that picture—the little girl who looked like Lucy Mae. When the light hit it just right she was Lucy, smiling sweetly at the big brother she loved. As hard as he tried, there was nothing in the world that could fill that void. "I love you, Lucy Mae," he whispered.

* * * * * * *

Reverend Churchill's voice droned from the radio. "Y'all come to our tabernacle now, y'here? We've got everything for the family. All that's needed to nurture their little spirits right here in downtown Oklahoma City. Sunday school and pot lucks, prayer meetings and penance, Boy Scout and Girl Scout troops all sponsored by your generous donations in the name of the Almighty."

"What's a Girl Scout, Momma?" Lucy Mae had asked.

"Nothin' but a bunch of dirty little girls in green dresses with nothin' better to do with their time."

"Can I be one? Please? It sounds fun...being with other girls."

"Fun is nothing but foolishness...and the devil can find little girls, even in churches."

Lucy didn't ask again.

But one day, in one of her kinder moments, Momma came home with an old Girl Scout uniform she had picked up in a thrift shop. She threw it at Lucy and said, "Here. This is as close as you're gonna get."

Lucy Mae loved her green dress and that was all she wore from that day forward.

Charlie awoke to a noise, like a muffled wind chime. He opened his eyes to a darkened room. The fire was dead and the cabin was meat locker cold. He exhaled as quietly as possible, listening intently for the source of the noise.

He heard it again.

Not wind chimes—more like metal—like his keys were being jostled where they lay on the dresser beside him. A noise like a sneak thief in the night.

He knew what it was.

Cunning little bastard, he thought. It was probably trying to take off with the whole damn key chain. And what was it planning to leave in its place? A pebble? A dead flower? A brass button or somebody's shiny new dime held safe in its nest for future trade?

Charlie Blackhawk hated pack rats.

He detested all sorts of fluffy, sneaky little things but he hated pack rats most of all. They would scurry into a room at night like felonious little smurfs, seeking their shiny treasures. They always left something in its place—like that didn't make it stealing at all! When Charlie stole, no one was left with the illusion that he had done them a favor. He damned well took what he wanted with no apologies.

He was entitled.

Pack rats, he thought, as him arm reached slowly outward. He cocked his head and listened intently. Following the rustling sound, his hand moved with the silence of a snake through the blades of darkness.

Wham!

It squealed and squirmed in Charlie's closed fist. His giggles and the pack rat's screams filled the room as he stumbled through the darkness into the kitchen.

"Gotcha this time, don't I, you fucking little fuzz ball?"

He held it tightly, tiny ribs cracking beneath his grasp, as his free hand searched the cupboard for a Mason jar. He held the jar, pushing it against his body with the hand that held the rat. His free hand unscrewed the lid.

Plop! Slam!

He re-screwed the lid as the sounds of frantic claws made a high-pitched scraping noise from inside the jar. Like fingernails on a blackboard. Or worn brake pads scraping against the bare metal of old brake drums. He shook the jar hard, like he was making a martini, then laughed as he set it on the counter. It took a few minutes for Charlie to find the kerosene lamp and fill it in the dark. (Gotta pay the electricity.) The lamp provided enough light for him to watch the pack rat as it flopped in terror, seeking a route of escape. But there was no escape. Charlie had it now.

He searched the cupboard for the old bottle. He always knew that bottle of chloroform would come in handy. He knew it on that long ago day when he had stolen it. There wasn't much that got past Charlie. He soaked a wad of toilet paper with some of the chloroform and shoved it into the jar. Then he replaced the lid tightly so that no air could enter. The pack rat jumped and screamed, dancing a frantic jig as it slammed against the glass. He watched it for a long time and as he watched his mind wandered. Lucy Mae and hot cigarettes and pretty little girls with skinny legs. As the pack rat twitched, he thought about his erection and what he wanted to do to make it better—to make it okay. He didn't want to be a bad boy, oh no, not Charlie. As the pack rat lay in death throes at the bottom of the jar, Charlie watched. And as he watched he thought about finding people for the watching games.... an alleyway in Hollywood...a pimp who had a stable that perfectly suited his tastes. And it was all only an hour and a half away.

Tomorrow he would take a little ride.

Charlie smiled as the helpless creature gasped a painful last breath. When he shook the jar the pack rat hit the sides with a thud. No more fighting. No more stealing what wasn't his. You don't NEVER take what's Charlie Blackhawk's. He continued to watch—as if he expected it to spring back to life.

But it didn't.

It didn't move at all.

He turned off the kerosene lamp and returned to the bare mattress. It smelled damp and felt cold against his body.

(It didn't move).

Charlie curled his body into a fetal position. Forbidden visions danced to a wild drum beat behind his closed eyelids, and he felt safe.

Charlie Blackhawk slept like a baby, but not for very long. He awoke restless. Tomorrow was too far away and he needed to do something about his gnawing thirst right now. He grabbed his car keys, bolted from the mattress, and slammed the door behind him.

CHAPTER THIRTEEN

Earlier that same day the school had called Jerry Hamill at the law firm. Unlike many lawyers who look forward to being high profile trial attorneys, Jerry found his comfort zone in the law library surrounded by the books. He shunned the spotlight, finding it an uncomfortable place to be. There was a balance and logic to the written word. A stability in the laws. So he did the painstaking research that gave fodder to the other attorneys so that they could grandstand before a jury, their captive audience. He furnished them with the laws as they were written and the precedents that would serve them best and they would twist them and distort them to suit their own purposes, in classic lawyer fashion.

Jerry had come home to wait for his daughter and before Amy arrived there had been yet another call. Amy had been seen digging up flowers from a neighbor's lawn.

It was after three-thirty when he heard the door slam. He walked into the hallway, scooping his daughter into his arms. "Hello, angel," he said.

"I love you, Daddy," she smiled, wrapping her arms around his neck.

"Amy, tell me about the flowers." He saw the confusion on her face and his heart ached as tears welled in her eyes. Her hands began to tremble as she choked on her response.

"I didn't mean to. I don't mean to be bad. Honest I don't. I...I, there was a girl, Daddy. She told me that she loved crocuses and that her mom wouldn't let her have them. I wanted to make her happy so I took them, but when I looked up she was gone." There was a long pause before she continued. "I really did see the girl," she said. "Oh Daddy, it's just getting worser and worser."

Jerry saw the dark circles under Amy's eyes and the worry-lines that crept across her face and he knew that he was no longer enough.

"The school called," he said. "They told me what happened in class today. I'm not upset with you, but I just don't know what to do any more. They have counselors, Amy. I wonder if talking to one of them might help you feel better."

She frowned as she thought about what he had suggested. "Okay," she finally said.

"And if you don't like it?"

"If they can help. I know I need help. I just don't know why this stuff happens."

"If you're really sure." He wasn't going to force it, but had already set an appointment for that same afternoon. Just in case. He was relieved she had agreed so easily. Amy was probably as desperate as Jerry was himself.

Later, as they were driving to the school, Amy said, "Mother said I'm crazy."

"You're not crazy."

"Then why are these awful things happening to me?"

* * * * * * *

Jerry Hamill felt uncomfortable. The chair was too small, child-sized, but that was not the only cause of his discomfort. He sat in the school psychologist's waiting room for what felt like an eternity, his eyes nervously scanning the room. The mint green paint was institutional, with a dusky, unclean glaze. The light wood doors were cheap and artificially grained, their surfaces plastic smooth. Amy had told him that the doors at school had monsters. He saw what she meant, for if he stared long enough distorted images emerged from the wood grain with gnomish faces, twisted branches, giraffes that stretched the length of the door. He would never have noticed the unnerving abstracts were it not for his daughter.

He turned his attention from the door, shifted his weight, then glanced impatiently at his Movado watch. His skin crawled with perspiration beneath its leather band. Jerry ran his fingers beneath the strap, circling around his wrist to alleviate the warm, damp itch. Amy had been in the psychologist's office for twenty-five minutes.

It was taking too long.

It was too quiet.

He disliked the woman already. When they had arrived, the petite, middle-aged woman had shaken his hand with an intimidating knuckle-buster grip—not what he would have expected from such a physically small female. Hardly the nurturing, grand-motherly type that he had expected. Instead he had come face to face with a Mack Truck bursting the confines of a two-cylinder chassis.

Then she had excluded him from the first session with a castrating dismissal.

Strike two. He did not like that at all.

He did not like leaving Amy alone with her.

Maybe he was being overly sensitive. Amy wanted help and this seemed the logical place to start. Doctors had been little help over the years, just repeating their "underdeveloped" mantra. Well, she was smart enough to pass in school, barely, and that was good enough for Jerry. She was fragile, that was all. But the dreams were another matter—they frightened her and he was unable to help. She had told him some of the dreams but insisted that others were too embarrassing to share.

So he hadn't pushed.

And now he didn't know what else to do but sit here and wait.

He didn't know what else to do. He felt ineffectual and that upset him.

The minutes stretched as slowly as thick rubber bands, then snapped.

A door slammed, jerking his attention to his right and the

source of the commotion. The noise had rattled him. He scowled as two strangers entered the room—a stocky woman with acned skin and an imitation leather briefcase noisily cleared her throat, then chugged with single-minded purpose across the room. A young policeman followed in her wake. They avoided eye contact with Jerry as the cop knocked on Mrs. Petroff's door.

They both went inside.

"What the...?" Jerry began.

"We will get to you shortly," Mrs. Petroff said, slamming the door with finality.

Jerry heard the lock tumble into place.

Something was very wrong. He stood up, ran to the closed door and pressed his ear against it, listening for snatches of conversation. But the sounds were too muffled, the voices too low. This was absurd. Five slow minutes passed. Then—"No." It was Amy's voice. "No!" He banged his fists on the door and pulled at the knob.

"What the hell is going on in there?" He kicked at the door. His hands shook. He felt hot tears on his face. The blood rushed and pounded at his temples. These strangers had made him helpless and he did not know why.

Why had a policeman been called?

"No!" Amy's voice was nearer—more panicked.

The door flew open and slammed against the wall. The policeman came out first, using his arm to block Jerry from reaching his daughter. The cop's features were soft, but his eyes darted nervously with the explosive potential of the situation. Jerry never thought he would see a cop as the enemy. Until now. It was all happening too fast and made no sense. The short woman came through the door next, holding Amy's arm tightly as the girl tried to free herself from her grip.

"You're hurting me," Amy said. "Daddy, she's hurting me."

Jerry tried to lunge toward Amy but the officer held firm.

"Everything will be fine," the woman was saying to Amy. "It will be safe now."

Amy stared back at the woman with the eyes of a terrorized

rabbit.

As Amy tried to reach for her father, the woman dragged her across the room and opened the door to the parking lot. Dust swirled in threads of late afternoon sun. Jerry blinked, adjusting his eyes to the sudden assault of daylight. He saw a second policeman beyond the door, older and stockier than the one who held him. This one scooped up Amy and carried her to the nearer of two parked squad cars. Amy's protestations filled the space between her father and herself—a space that lengthened like the murky afternoon shadows.

"I can't believe this!" Jerry said, attempting to push past the first officer. The policeman held him by the shoulders as Jerry tried to push his weight through the young man. It didn't work.

"Just calm down," the cop said, resisting the temptation to pull his revolver, knowing it would only escalate the situation. "Please, let's not make this more difficult than it has to be."

From through the open door Jerry saw the woman open the rear door of the squad car and get in. The second policeman placed Amy in the woman's lap. The door slammed shut. The cop walked briskly to the driver's side, opened the door, then got behind the wheel.

The car door slammed.

The engine started.

The cop threw the car into reverse, jerked it into first, hit the gas, and peeled out.

Amy was gone.

"What the hell's going on here?" Jerry directed his words to Mrs. Petroff, who had maintained a stoic silence through it all. "For God's sake, we came here for help and you've given us chaos. What the hell are you doing?"

"Protecting that child."

"Protecting her from what? You have no right to do this."

"I am quite within my rights, Mr. Hamill," she said calmly. "My obligation is the welfare of that poor child."

Jerry felt light-headed but pulled away from the policeman's loosened grip. "What exactly are you implying?" He asked, but sensed the answer before the words completed forming on his lips. The policeman finally released his hold but kept his eyes on Jerry.

"I have every reason to believe," Petroff began, "every indication that Amy is the victim of abuse."

His thoughts ran faster than he could catch them, but "That's just crazy," was all he could manage.

"Is it? That is precisely what we intend to find out. She has been released to the custody of Social Services."

"She needs my protection, not yours. She needs my strength. Her mother's gone and—damn you, I'm all that she has. You can't do this...."

"Oh, yes we can. We protect the child, not the offending parent. A medical examination will...."

"No...."

"...determine if our suspicions are correct."

"You are so wrong!"

"I sincerely hope so."

"But I'm guilty until proven innocent, is that it? In her desperation to be strong, she agreed to come to you. It was an act of courage on her part, but instead of helping all you did was frighten her even more. You did that, not me. As her father I have rights."

"Just calm down," said the policeman.

"When abuse is suspected you forfeit those rights," Mrs. Petroff said. "You're a lawyer—you most certainly should know the law."

"This is bullshit!" He spun around, paced the length of the room. Perspiration burned his eyes. The room was stifling. His dress shirt clung to his back as he raised his arm to wipe his eyes with his shirt sleeve.

"We are done," she said with finality. "The Department of Social Services will contact you once their investigation is completed."

"And then?"

"Either she will be returned to you or she will not. If she is not it will be for good reason and you will face charges of child molestation and abuse. That's the law—live with it."

"Let's go," the officer said.

Jerry walked toward the open door, then turned. "I did nothing," he said. "Sometimes the system is wrong. I would never hurt my little girl. They're not protecting her—they're making it worse. She'll feel abandoned. Again."

He exited to where he had parked his car, opened the door and slid in. He stared ahead, trying to regain his composure, to clear his head. How, he wondered, could one little woman have wreaked such havoc so swiftly? He composed his thoughts as the shadows of tall eucalyptus trees stretched across the empty parking lot.

His world had grown dark.

Hating Mrs. Petroff served no purpose. Her mind was made up. Probably before they had ever arrived.

The Social Worker was just doing her job.

The cops were doing their jobs.

I'll go to the office and clear up this mess before the sun sets, he told himself, and Amy will be home where she belongs, asleep in her own bed.

Safe.

CHAPTER FOURTEEN

Jan Smith looked out the window. From where she sat at her favorite booth at the Wagon Wheel she could see the General Store. The dreary day had depressed her. Silver frost shimmered on the heavy branch-tips of the pines and the landscape was shrouded in thick fog. She was eager for summer and her "sunshine strangers", as she called them. Summer visitors who would show her a good time and move on—no strings, no gossip.

That was as high as expectations got at Pine Lake.

The chill air pushed through the window causing her nipples to stand at attention. (Itty-bitty-titty, that was what some local jerk-off had called her.) Damn, she could sure use somebody more sophisticated than these yokels—even if it was just for play time. She reached for her sweater where it lay in the booth next to her. She leaned toward the window as she pulled on a sleeve—and spotted the car.

Pushing her arm through the other sleeve, she watched as the old Chevy Nova, license plate HAWK, exited the side road and turned onto the main drag. She smiled, remembering that he had laid in a week's worth of groceries. She would catch him when he came back up the hill.

After all, "Sunshine strangers" were as scarce as freckles on grizzly bears this time of year.

* * * * * * *

Charlie Blackhawk descended the mountain, leaving the fog at higher altitudes. A layer of ochre-tinged pollution hovered over San Bernardino and Redlands. San Bernardino—San Berdoo—Berdoo—The Flats...Mountain folk's names for the city. Charlie drove right through Berdoo. He was on his way to Hollywood—to the watching games—and he was in a hurry.

* * * * * * *

Charlie awoke parked on the shoulder of a desert road, disoriented. Two beef jerky wrappers sat on the seat. He didn't remember pulling over and was momentarily confused. He blinked his eyes, then remembered where he was headed. He got out of the car to stretch his legs before continuing on his journey.

"Hoo-wee!" he yelled into the emptiness.

Charlie Blackhawk stood as still as the desert yuccas—tall and foreboding and evil. The desert possessed a particular warmth for Charlie as he surveyed its vastness. His heart lifted to near-elation as he gazed upon the last splashes of orange-purple hues that whispered through the darkness. He felt utter joy as silent lizards scurried across the desert floor.

He was remembering....

...twisted metal,

...and a child's limp body lying in a back seat.

Charlie laughed aloud at a speeding roadrunner. He heard the psalms of airborne angels on the lonely wind, and the unforgiving sands made his heart rejoice.

(The woman's neck had made a scrunching sound when he'd broken it.)

"Hoo-wee!"

He felt in control again.

* * * * * * *

Jerry Hamill had succeeded. For now. Being an attorney with

an important law firm had its advantages. And knowing a few judges never hurt. The right papers got signed and Amy was returned to his custody. It was not the end of the matter, by a long shot, but at least she was home where she belonged instead of scared to death in some foster home.

Amy sat on the floor of her room. A Monopoly board sat between her and Freddy, with most of the money on his side. As usual.

"Are you sure you want to keep playing?" he said.

"Oh, yes."

"But you always lose."

"Maybe I'll win this time," she said. Freddy shifted his weight from one plump hip to the other then pushed up his glasses as they slid down the bridge of his nose. Her friend read her thoughts.

"Don't let it bother you so much, Amy. Adults screw up lots of stuff. Sometimes they just aren't as smart as they want us to think."

* * * * * * *

Charlie Blackhawk found his way back to the main road and headed toward Hollywood. He lit a Camel, coughing as he inhaled. He turned the radio full blast.

Dolly Parton sang in her sweet, lilting twang.

"Slut!" Charlie screamed. (Stay away from those harlots, his mother's voice whispered, stay away.) Charlie slammed his fist against the radio knob. The car was silent. "I'm invisible, invisible, invisible," he muttered. "Can't find me here."

HIDDEN MEADOWS NEXT EXIT, the sign read.

And Charlie drove on into the night.

* * * * * * *

From through the upstairs window of a house on the street named Avenida Larkspur, in the community of Hidden

Meadows, came a little girl's scream.

She screamed and screamed, and her terror filled the darkness.

* * * * * * *

In the small house in Hollywood, Meg Stinson handed a drink to her agent. Jason Mittleman sat, knees tightly locked, in an uncomfortable kitchen chair as Meg paced the room.

"You sent me on three interviews today and I was hit on twice. If you want to be my agent, I expect you to protect me. I've had enough of those vultures." She was getting increasingly fed up with the whole business.

"Take my advise," Jason said. "You're sexy—hit them over the head with it."

"I will *not* sleep with them!"

"I'm not telling you to sleep with them. Stop being so damn defensive. Just tease them, let them feel they *might* get lucky. Play your assets and you'll have them eating out of your hand. You're are a big girl now, Meg. You know how to say no, just stop being so paranoid."

Meg twisted a finger through her blonde hair. "Do I sound paranoid?"

"Yes, you do."

"Well, they really are after me." She laughed.

"So who wouldn't be?"

* * * * * * *

Betty sat in her bed, pillows propped behind her large body. She was trying to read but was also straining to hear the conversation between Meg and Jason in the other room. She rooted for her friend's success but worried about losing her in the process. Both Meg and Sabrina were more to her than people who shared a space. They had become her friends. Her family. She sighed, turned the page of her romance novel, and read on.

* * * * * * *

Charlie Blackhawk swerved the Nova to the right, exiting at Highland Avenue. The Hollywood Bowl was unlit. He drove past Hollywood Boulevard and made a turn onto Melrose Avenue. It was late and Charlie was anxious. His hands trembled against the steering wheel as a lunatic giggle escaped from through his clenched teeth.

* * * * * * *

Sabrina Stinson sat at Miss Cooney's bedside. Her auburn hair fell forward as she reached for the old woman's hand, cupping it in her own. Miss Cooney opened her lids, delicate as Japanese rice paper, and smiled. The corners of her mouth quivered and a milky haze covered her eyes. Without surgery, she would soon be blind. And an eighty-eight year old woman was a poor candidate for any kind of surgery.

She would miss Sabrina's animated face.

"I should go," said Sabrina. "It's getting late."

"Did you bring the merchandise?" said Miss Cooney, feigning a sinister air. Her eyes twinkled mischievously, even through the cataracts.

Sabrina stood, looked around the room, then reached into her pocket. She pulled out the Oh Henry® and placed it in the old woman's hand.

"Mission accomplished," Sabrina winked.

* * * * * * *

A gaudy, neon sign flickered: STARLET MOTEL. Charlie Blackhawk pulled into the parking lot and checked in. As he walked through the shadows toward his room, reflections from the sign washed across his grinning face, painting it in the hues of darkest blue and in reds the color of blood.

Later that night, in the neon-splashed darkness, Charlie

Blackhawk walked alone. The streets of Hollywood reeked of corruption and he inhaled the fetid essence with glee. He felt like a child in a candy store as he walked the length of Hollywood Boulevard, studying the vacant eyes of the night dwellers. Young girls, painted like sad Pierrots, wore tight shorts and wobbled as awkwardly as newborn colts as they attempted to strut in high heeled shoes.

They excited Charlie. He would look at their skinny, child's legs—imagine spreading them—dream of his ensuing punishments.

He walked alone and dreamed of the wrath of someone else's god—his mother's god. He thought of the price he would inflict upon himself for tonight's sins. He dreamed of knives and razor blades and hot, burning embers and as his fantasies crescendoed his erection grew stiff beneath his Levis.

* * * * * * *

That same night Amy Hamill had a nightmare. In it a man knelt before a young girl and a woman in a leather mask. The man was crying and begging the woman to punish him. She beat him with a belt, raising welts across his back and legs as he cowered naked at her feet. Blood trickled down his thighs.

The young girl sat on the edge of the bed, staring blankly, as if nothing were wrong.

"It's time for the watching game," the man said in a child's voice as he rose to sit next to the girl on the bed. He lit a cigarette. He inhaled the smoke deeply and lowered the hot cigarette to his nakedness. He was smiling.

The girl and the woman watched in silence as the man laughed and sobbed.

Amy was horrified by the vision. It was obscene and frightening. Then the man looked up and she saw his eyes.

She woke up screaming.

She screamed and screamed. She screamed until her voice grew tight and she could scream no more.

Over and over again, she muttered the same word: "Danger, danger, danger," in a mindless, babbling chant.

CHAPTER FIFTEEN

Sabrina Stinson and her mother, Meg, unloaded the cartons of Girl Scout Cookies from the back of the old Volkswagen. Sabrina waved to three other girls who were already set up in front of the Safeway. Today was their last-ditch effort to sell the remainder of their inventory. Lemon Pastry Cremes—Caramel Delights—Shortbread Cookies. The favorite flavors had already sold out. And Sabrina, Meg, and Betty had finished the last three boxes of Chocolate Chip themselves. "Let's eat up the profits," Betty had squealed, and they had gobbled them down guiltlessly the night before while watching The Best of Johnny Carson.

The occasional ray of sunshine tore hesitantly through the clouded, unforgiving sky. The early morning chill would soon give way to a warmer day. Then people would come in droves to do their weekend shopping. Better to catch them on their way into the store while they still had money in their pockets, Sabrina thought. Hardly anyone said yes on the way out. Once their carts were filled and their pockets were running on empty they pretended they didn't see you standing there—or they mumbled something about dieting even as packs of Oreos peeked out from the tops of their filled to bursting grocery bags.

Standing out here peddling cookies was not her idea of a fun-filled Saturday, but it had been her idea, after all. Only the three other girls and their mothers had shown up and Sabrina had hoped for a better turn out. This was her chance to show off Meggie. It was the selling part she didn't like—having to outsmart people all the time—it was annoying. But it was another game and Sabrina was good at games. Adults could be such liars, even to little kids. Well, she wasn't little any more, but still. The grown-ups would either buy or feed her bullshit, in which case Sabrina would hustle them all the way to their cars. Nothing to lose—either she sold a box or they lost their cool. It was very uncool to yell at a Girl Scout, at which point she would look down sadly and likely end up with a guilt sale.

She was a good little game player.

Sabrina looked up to see what had blocked the morning light. A rain cloud? A tall, tanned man stood before her. He wore an odd expression she could not identify. Warmth? Sadness? She could not tell for sure, but it looked out of place on his rugged face. As he removed his sunglasses she looked into eyes that melted like quicksilver. She couldn't tell if he was looking straight at her or not...or through her...or past her. There was a distance to his voice as he spoke—his words were strung together but sounded as disconnected as a riddle. She felt as if it was not really her he was speaking to at all.

"I would sure like some Peanut Butter Patties. I'll buy all you've got, little sister."

"I've only got Mint Patties, mister, and plenty of Caramels and Shortbreads. Is that okay?"

The man did not answer but Sabrina read the disappointment on his face.

"Would that be alright? The Mints and the Shortbreads?"

"Don't you remember me?" he mumbled.

"What did you say?" She wasn't sure if she had heard him right. "I couldn't hear you."

"Sure. That would be just fine," he said with a smile.

Meg Stinson walked over to where her daughter stood. "Do you need some help?" she asked, not sure if she was addressing the man or Sabrina.

"I just wasn't sure what he wanted. We're out of the peanut butter ones." Sabrina said.

"Why, is this your little girl?" Charlie asked. Meg nodded.

"She is almost as pretty as her mother. I was just telling her I would like to buy up all the cookies she has left. I've got a real sweet tooth this morning."

He turned on the charm. He assessed the woman and wished he hadn't worn his boots. This was a real lady, no shit-kicking trailer trash he could wind around his little finger. She would take a special approach. Momma would have called her "uptown." She had told him about their blood being different, blue or something, but he had spilled enough blood in his travels to know they all bled the same. (The poor shall always be among us, she had said, the rich will always see to that.)

Was that from the bible?

Sometimes Momma confused him so.

He watched as the Girl Scout and the uptown lady put the boxes of cookies into a larger box. He looked at the lady's hand. She wore no wedding band. He counted the money and handed it to the pretty young girl, all the time being careful to make eye contact with the mother.

"Thanks. We have to be going." Meg handed him the box and turned to leave.

"Ma'am, perhaps I could give you both a lift."

Oh, you're a stupid shit, Charlie Blackhawk thought. How the hell do you expect to impress a lady with that old Nova? You stupid, stupid dumb ass.

Meg looked up at the tall man. He reminded her of an old-time movie star—Randolph Scott in his prime perhaps—handsome and weather-worn like a hero from some old western oater. The lone stranger who rode in on a horse as white as his Stetson to tame some wild, lawless town. Nice to look at, sure. But he was a man nonetheless. Sidney Newhouse—Junior Barnes—they were all the same. But the warning alarm that went off in Meg's head went unheeded as she and Sabrina started the walk to their car.

Junior had returned to the motel room later that night, awakening her from a restless sleep. He turned her onto her stomach with a rough jerk (you'll learn to please a man). He beat her with his fists (she learned real fast for a kid). She was resigned.

Look Mom, Mary Margaret's a big girl now.

Innocence was dead.

Junior Barnes was no savior, no hero, but he was one hell of a teacher.

Her fall from grace was complete but she had a long way to go before she hit rock bottom.

"Thanks for the offer," she said to the man, "but we have a car. Enjoy the cookies."

"Yeah, thanks," Sabrina pitched in.

"Char...Charles Black's the name."

"Well, thanks Charles, but we really must be going."

You won't get rid of me that easy, you uppity cunt, Charlie thought as he turned toward his car. He looked back and saw them get into a battered Volkswagen, but they did not see him. Hell, they didn't give him a second look. He had been dismissed. The Invisible Man. He hopped into the Nova and turned the key in the ignition.

Neither Meg nor Sabrina noticed as the old Nova lagged a block behind them. They were talking excitedly about Friday's Hollywood Reporter and Gideon Stark's mention of Meg in his column. "A new face and a fiery talent," he had said. Meg had not given him a second thought at Tony Savage's party, but apparently her argument with Sidney had made quite an impression. They had bought ten copies of the Reporter and pasted a page on the refrigerator door. Betty had highlighted the comments with a bright pink marker.

Then they had opened a bottle of cheap Andre champagne.

Later that day Meg's agent called. The interviews had already begun. Maybe there was some justice in the world after all. Somebody else could give Newhouse his blow-jobs and she would finally have parts with more than two lines.

The Nova followed at a cautious distance, Charlie watching as the Volkswagen pulled into the driveway. He pulled to the curb half a block back and watched them enter the small wood-frame house. You can't get rid of Charlie Blackhawk that easy, he thought as he opened a box of Thin Mints and popped one into his mouth. They didn't taste as good as Peanut Butter Patties but he was good at pretending and pretty soon he could feel the peanut butter on the roof of his mouth.

He had found Lucy Mae, that was the important thing. He had not even been thinking about her and all of a sudden there she was, right in front of him. Maybe she had really found him this time, had been looking for him all along.

Charlie Blackhawk sat behind the wheel for a long time, eating Mint Cookies that tasted just like peanut butter and thinking.

Thinking real, real hard.

CHAPTER SIXTEEN

"We could have put Amy in McLaren Hall or foster care...in a safe environment, until this matter is resolved. Do you really think pulling strings was the best thing for *her?* I have seen you lawyers in action more times than I care to count—children being returned to abusive homes only to be molested again—or worse. It is the legal system that fails these kids. I'm going to nail you, Mr. Hamill. We're going to find the proof we need to prevent her from ever being returned to you again."

Jerry had won the battle so far—he had Amy back home. Pulling strings and using his connections were all the ammunition he had to fight with. The woman who stood before him had short-cropped black hair, a dark suit with a man's shirt and tie. He saw an angry woman blinded by her own prejudices as she championed a legitimate cause, a cause Jerry himself felt strongly about.

But he had already been judged.

"Not all men are evil," he said. "I would never victimize my own daughter. I would never victimize anyone."

The woman shuffled her papers. "Ms. Flores's initial report says your daughter has all the classic signs...."

"For instance?"

"The fears, the nightmares, the bed-wetting, sexual knowledge beyond her years. Need I continue?"

"The doctor's report said she is intact. Doesn't that indicate you are on the wrong track here?"

"I could spend hours reciting horror stories of abuses perpetrated on girls who remain intact," she snapped. "Men can be very clever, very imaginative. Believe me, Mr. Hamill, this investigation is far from over. As things proceed you are to continue Amy's sessions with Ms. Flores. And put this on the record—one out of four girls are sexually molested—one out of four! The statistics speak for themselves."

There was no point in arguing with the woman. They would see Ms. Flores, no problem. The important thing was that he had Amy with him while the system spun its wheels.

* * * * * * *

"Don't hit me so hard, Momma," Charlie had begged as his mother's fist made contact with the side of his head. "It makes my head feel bad. It makes it hurt even when you aren't hitting me."

Charlie's brain was fuzzy when he heard the knock on the door. It was only 11 A.M. but Charlie needed to work things off so he could function. He was formulating a plan. He opened the door and a woman stood before him, holding the hand of a young girl. The girl was wearing a cheap red wig, just as he had ordered, and she looked up at the woman nervously.

"Magic sent us," the woman said.

"Magic?"

"Yeah, Magic—The Magic Man," she said as they entered the motel room. She seemed agitated as she undressed herself. Beads of perspiration dotted her brow despite the room's chill. Charlie explained the rules of the game as the woman wiped her arm across her forehead. Festering track marks raged across her clammy skin and her hands trembled as she undressed the girl.

When Charlie stepped out of his jeans the girl gasped.

"Get on the bed and pretend you are sleeping," he said.

The girl froze, her arms folded to cover her undeveloped breasts.

"Just do what he says and we'll be outta here," the woman said. A high-pitched urgency punctuated her words as she absently rubbed the marks on her arm. She needed a fix. *Badly.*

"Mommy!" The girl said, but she obeyed and lay stiffly on one of the beds, her eyes squeezed tightly shut.

Charlie lay on the other bed and grinned as the woman mounted him, a cigarette dangling from her mouth, as ordered.

"Say it," he snapped.

"You be a good boy and mind your momma."

"That's good," he said as he slid inside of her. His gaze was intense as he watched the woman grind her pelvis against his groin.

Ten-year-old Charlie lay in fear on his bed, awaiting the punishment from God that his mother was obligated to inflict upon him. God had told her so. The hot embers from her cigarette seared the young flesh of his penis, shooting the pain through his body. Pain and pleasure intertwined, sending their mixed messages to his impressionable mind.

Pain and pleasure.

Again, the woman straddled him.

"You been a bad boy," she repeated.

"Now say it!" Charlie yelled, sliding out of her, unable to maintain his erection. "Say it."

"I...."

"Say it, you stupid twat."

"I...I want to watch you with her." The woman's trembling finger pointed to the young girl on the bed.

The girl looked up, eyes wide.

"I don't want to," said Charlie, but he got into the bed next to her, his hands prying apart her unyielding thighs. His hand slid up her leg, cupping her hairless mound. His breathing was shallow and rapid as his hands hesitantly toyed with her.

"Lucy Mae," he whispered.

He grabbed the girl by her wrists and knelt over her, pushing her legs apart with his knee. In one swift movement he fell atop her, pressing his semi-erection against her, unable to drive himself into her. Instantaneously, a pained moan escaped through his lips. "Nooooo."

"Mommy no!" the girl screamed. Her screams turned to sobs and her sobs slapped Charlie to the present. He rolled off of her, bolted from the bed, slapped the woman hard across the face.

"Stupid bitch!" he yelled, "You made her cry. Look, you hurt her and made her cry. You didn't play the game right, fucked it all up, didn't say the words when you were supposed to."

"I...I'm sorry, I'll do it right this time." The woman touched the painful welts raising across her cheek.

"It's too late," he said. Then, in an anguished child's voice he added: "Made her cry you hurt her and made her cry bad mother made my Lucy cry." His fingers recoiled into fists and his fists covered his ears as he attempted to block out the girl's sobs. "Didn't mean to hurt you Lucy," he whined. "Didn't mean to Lucy love you Lucy love you Momma made me do it Lucy Lucy Lucy."

His head snapped around, his eyes fixed intently on the woman. "Get the fuck out of here. Tell Magic or The Magic Man or whatever the hell you call him to send someone who knows how to play the game."

The woman was going to tell Charlie that he had to pay her—that Magic would be pissed off—that he would not send anyone else unless Charlie paid her now , but as she opened her mouth to speak she looked into Charlie's rabid eyes and knew to say nothing.

The Magic Man would have to collect on this one himself.

CHAPTER SEVENTEEN

With the patience of a vulture, Charlie Blackhawk sat perched atop the Nova. It was early afternoon and he was getting hungry. For nearly an hour he watched, and waited. He smoked one Camel after another while he waited and watched the cars come and go.

The Van Nuys parking lot for the Airport Flyaway Bus Service was large. It was a secure place to leave one's car and take the bus to LAX; so much easier than fighting the bumper to bumper Los Angeles traffic to the International Airport.

Safe.

Unless Charlie Blackhawk was in town.

Waiting patiently for just the right one, Charlie watched. When the Sterling pulled into a space two rows down his muscles twitched. Things were looking good. As a man opened his door the little brats' whining spilled across the blacktop. Little boys were just not nice like little girls, Charlie thought. Little boys were bad, bad, bad.

Charlie knew all about bad little boys.

A raspy chuckle escaped from Charlie's throat as he watched the man struggle with the luggage. Charlie did not need a formal education to read people. He hopped off the hood, flicking his cigarette through the air. Smog stained the valley a doleful amber and unseasonable heat soaked his underarms. Ass holes, he thought, sauntering over to where the man fought his overload. Good Samaritan Charlie offered to assist.

The man smiled and Charlie stood silent as the trunk slammed shut. The man shoved car keys into his left jacket pocket. The two men picked up the suitcases and walked to the bus terminal.

"Thank you for the help," the wife said. Between the car and the line Charlie had learned all he needed to know. They would be in England for two weeks and that gave Charlie plenty of time.

People pushed against each other as they edged towards the waiting bus, kicking their suitcases ahead of them with their feet as they jostled and inched their way forward. Seeing his opportunity, Charlie purposely lunged forward and tripped over a suitcase, catching himself as he fell against the man that he had helped from the parking lot. He apologized, wished the family a safe trip, then waved them off. As he walked away he felt deep inside his pocket, his fingers curled around the keys to the Sterling. They would be half way to Gatwick before the fool would notice they were gone. He would probably figure he had dropped them when he got out of his car. It would give his wife a reason to admonish him. Probably in front of the kids and strangers. Ass holes. Everything was working out just hunky-dory.

Charlie walked back to the Nova and opened the trunk. He pulled out New Mexico plates, personal belongings and a dusty bottle of chloroform then headed across the lot to the Sterling.

His Sterling.

* * * * * * *

Charlie could not remember how long he had been parked in the Hollywood Hills, but it was nightfall. He was fairly sure that no more than half a day had passed, but he could not be certain. Sometimes hours slipped away, sometimes entire days, when he was thinking. Time seemed to slide in and out of reality like Charlie himself. Ordinarily the passage of time meant little to him, but now he had a mission to fulfill.

He had seen the vision and it spoke to him in riddles, but he had grasped the meaning. The child's prayers would be answered. He sat in the Sterling with its New Mexico plates and lit smoke after smoke. It helped him focus. The city lay in neon throbs beneath him and a soft breeze whispered shameful tales in his ears from through the eucalyptus branches above.

Charlie felt in control of all that lay beneath him. He resisted the urge to masturbate in the darkness, for if all went well there would be such wondrous games to play.

Games...was that the plan?

Or was it something else?

He could not remember. But it would be soon.

Very soon now.

Oh, so very soon.

CHAPTER EIGHTEEN

Sabrina sat in the darkened living room, eyes glued to *The Great Escape* on the television. Charles Bronson had his first really big role in this movie and she would not have missed it for anything. He had changed his name from Buchinsky to Bronson for political reasons at a time when ethnic names, especially anything than rang Russian or Eastern European, raised *red* flags. She did not look up as Betty walked through the front door. "Some days suck," Betty said. "And you shouldn't be watching in the dark. It's bad for your eyes."

"It's *The Great Escape*."

"Want ice cream?" They went to the kitchen, dished it out and returned to the television just as Bronson crawled through the claustrophobic tunnel, muscled arms gritty with dirt and slick with perspiration.

"Total hunk," said Sabrina.

"Totally," Betty mimicked. "Hell, I'd settle for John Candy."

"Meg is still out on interviews but I made a big tuna casserole. She worries me, Betty. Jason pushes too hard—she's flying on pure adrenaline and already headed for burnout. This is really too much pressure. Maybe too much despite the possible rewards, don't you think?"

"He believes in her, honey. We all do—more than she believes in herself I fear."

Betty arose from the couch, hoisting the elastic waistband up on her slacks as she headed for the kitchen. She hated fat girl clothes, as well as the constant shortness of breath. But she loved her food. It filled a void, she knew that, but it worked. She leaned over the oven door and took out the casserole, setting it atop the stove. The phone hung on the wall above the utensil drawer. She fished through the silverware, steak knives and butcher knives, and pulled out a large spoon. Everything was tossed into the drawer with no semblance of order. As bad as a house full of bachelors, she thought, spooning the casserole into bowls, knowing the portions would not appease her appetite, knowing hunger pains would soon undermine the best of intentions. She sighed as she returned to sit next to Sabrina on the couch. She handed her a bowl, and they began to eat, eyes fixed on the television screen. And Bronson.

* * * * * * *

Amy got tired early that night. She pulled on her flannel nighty and crawled into bed, happy she was home. She kept the light on. The darkness had become her enemy. And when she slept the dreams came. She was exhausted, but fought the urge to close her heavy lids. Despite her efforts, her eyes soon closed and she began to drift. Aware that she was slipping away, she forced her eyes open and stared at the light. Finally her eyes closed again. The sandman had won.

And the dreams came.

But, for once, the dreams were beautiful visions that granted her peaceful sleep. She saw a beautiful girl with flowing auburn hair. The girl danced in a field of flowers and when she laughed, Amy laughed with her. When the girl twirled, Amy twirled— when she leaped, Amy followed like a mirror image through the wrong end of a telescope. The girl bent to pick crocus blossoms and when Amy bent down their eyes met.

And Amy knew her and she knew Amy, and when they hugged it felt as if two pieces of an interlocking jigsaw puzzle were fitting perfectly into place.

The image caused Amy to smile in her sleep.

* * * * * * *

Perhaps because of the darkness, Meg Stinson did not notice the black Sterling as it followed her to the Safeway. Her mind was on getting home and cheap Andre Champagne and long-distance phone calls and memories she strained to keep buried. She shoveled dirt over those memories, pulled into a parking space, turned off the ignition, and went inside the store.

"If this isn't a fine coincidence," the voice said, circling around her from behind. She did not look as she continued to shove oranges into a brown sack.

"Surely you remember me," the voice said. Was he speaking to her? She turned and looked into the tanned face with its patchwork lines. Something was familiar, like an old-time western hero. She held the oranges against her chest, blonde hair tumbling forward as she moved.

"This morning," the man continued. "I bought the Girl Scout Cookies, remember?"

"Sure. Hi," she said, forcing a smile as she turned the cart away from him.

"I thought maybe...."

She pretended not to hear him as she pushed the cart away and entered the next aisle. The wheels wobbled as she tried to steer a straight line, hoping he wouldn't follow. Men made her uneasy. In the frozen food aisle she looked up and there he was again, determined to hold her attention.

His voice was soft and gentle. "I've been here on business and hoped you might want to join me, you and your daughter...."

"Sorry, I do not date."

"We don't have all these great sights back in...New Mexico. It just don't—doesn't seem right going alone but I am downright determined to see a few things before I head back on Monday. I thought maybe...."

"No, not interested." But she was weakening. He was polite, well-dressed. *Cowboy boots. Why did she keep thinking about cowboy boots?* This man was knits and tweeds, and everything he wore looked brand new. She detected the faint aroma of Irish Spring. Okay, he certainly seemed harmless enough. But still.

"No. No, I'm sorry." She headed for the check-out line.

The parking lot lights cast long shadows that followed Meg as she pushed her cart to the car. She sat the heavy brown bag of groceries on the roof of her car while she searched her purse for her keys.

The black Sterling rolled silently into the empty space next to Meg's Volkswagen. Out of the corner of her eye she could not help but notice the shiny car. Maybe some day she could trash her old heap for something nice like that. The interviews were rolling in and it was encouraging. And dreams were a new luxury. They were already pushing away the dark clouds, if only in intervals. But it was a start. *You'll be driving a fucking Ferrari! Isn't that what Jason had said?*

"Just one more try," came the voice from the Sterling, the voice of the man from inside the store.

"Don't you ever give up?"

Here on business he had said. Be gone Monday. What would be the harm?

"No strings?"

"No strings," Charlie Blackhawk promised. "Charles Black's the name." Easy as pushing out abscessed teeth with root-rot, he thought to himself, just gotta know where to apply the pressure.

"Meg Stinson. And my daughter is Sabrina. No time for sightseeing, sorry, but Sunday is her birthday if you would like to join us to celebrate. Nothing fancy. Just a small daytime get-together at our house."

"Sabrina, what a pretty name," Charlie said, but he knew she was lying. Why, her name was not Sabrina at all.

Meg scribbled her address on the cash register receipt and handed it to Charlie.

"Until tomorrow then," he smiled.

* * * * * * *

That night Sabrina lay in bed staring at the ceiling. In her mind's eye she found herself tying and untying the knots that had earned her a merit badge. Tying and untying them and trying to remember their names and uses. Before long she felt herself floating, like she had on that other night, floating high above her body and looking down, seeing herself on the bed below. This time it wasn't as frightening. She had told Betty about it and Betty, well-read as she was, told her that she'd read a book once about something called *astral traveling*. That it was a gift some people were just blessed with. Sabrina would have written it off as just so much bullshit voodoo, like reading Tarot cards and telling fortunes from the lines on someone's palm— had she not experienced it herself.

So when it happened again, she felt awe rather than fear.

She was not going to panic.

Not this time.

This time she willed herself to the bedroom door and beyond, all the way to Betty's room. She knew she had a gift if she could learn to control it. The need to be in control was strong in Sabrina, perhaps because everything around her so lacked structure. Their entire lifestyle was more suited to a loft in Greenwich Village back in the beatnik days.

Control was important. It helped to mold things into the right places.

Her form floated above the doorway of Betty's room. She concentrated hard and soon propelled herself above Betty's bed. Sabrina listened to Betty's heavy breathing, rattling like an asthmatic child as she slept unaware beneath the girl's hovering form,

and then,

THUD!

Sabrina was in her bed again.

"Shit!" Next time, she told herself, next time I will not let that happen. Next time I will be in control.

Meggie was sleeping restfully at her side as Sabrina fell into a deep sleep. She did not awaken until mid-morning and when she awoke she was a year older.

It was Sunday and it was her birthday.

* * * * * * *

Late the previous night there was a loud banging on the motel room door. Charlie pulled back the curtain to see who it was. Nobody knew he was here. It took a minute for things to register. It was the pimp. The Magic Man.

Charlie left the chain on the door and opened it a crack.

"What the hell do you want?"

"Let me in."

"Get lost. Go away."

"There be something we needs to discuss. Let me in."

Hesitantly, Charlie undid the chain and opened the door. The Magic Man was almost half the height of Charlie, who nearly filled the doorway as The Magic Man pushed past him and entered the room.

"We have gots a small problem we need to take care of," he said.

"And what's that?" Charlie had his antenna up and smelled trouble.

"You failed to pay that fine lady I sent to you this morning."

"She screwed everything up, Magic. I told her the rules and she messed it all up. She nearly hurt that sweet little girl. She didn't earn a fucking dime."

"You still gotta pay for her time. For *their* time. You think that was an easy order to fill?"

"No way."

The Magic Man pulled out a gun, which certainly added some clout to his lack of stature, and aimed it at the center of Charlie's forehead. "Let's be reasonable about this," said the pimp.

Damn, I wish you hadn't done that, Charlie thought. I really wish you hadn't.

" Okay, okay, as long as you put it that way," he said. "Just cool it and I'll get your fucking money."

Charlie turned from the pimp and walked over to the night stand, picking up his wallet. He could still feel the gun aimed at his back. He turned and walked back to where The Magic Man stood, still aiming at him—staring at him with his shifty, intense eyes.

"Hey, no hard feelings," Charlie said as he rifled through his wallet and took out the money. "Let's just settle this. How much did you say?"

The pimp changed his focus to the money which Charlie held in front of him. He had diverted his attention just long enough for Charlie to grab the gun. He punched the pimp in the gut, hard, and as the man doubled over in surprise and pain, Charlie landed an uppercut which caught the man off balance and he fell on his back onto the carpet. Charlie pinned him down and reached over for a bed pillow, placing it over his face. He wanted to strangle him with his bare hands. He liked the feel of doing things up close, but this guy was a wiry little shit and much stronger than Charlie had anticipated. No time for a scuffle. It was not worth taking the chance of being overpowered, unlikely as that prospect might be. Or for the man to recapture the gun. Or to give him the chance to make any unnecessary noise.

Charlie lifted the gun and shoved it against the pillow, squeezing off one good shot into The Magic Man's head. One less pimp in the world. But the result was pretty damn bloody and Charlie liked things tidy. This was one of the reasons he hated guns. There was always a mess. The pillow had muffled the sound, hopefully enough that it did not draw any attention.

He waited a long time, sitting next to the body bleeding out on the floor. No commotion. No knocks on the door. It was the middle of the night and if anyone had heard a gunshot, it had gone ignored.

He looked out the window several times. The parking area was devoid of people.

When he felt it was safe, he rolled the pimp into a blanket and threw him into the trunk of the car.

Charlie drove the alleyways of Hollywood. It was dark and quiet except for the occasional drunk—or faggot on the prowl—or crack whore looking to turn one last trick.

Damn, but he loved this town.

He turned into an unlit alley, pulled up next to a dumpster behind a restaurant, then looked around before opening the trunk. The dumpster was overloaded with trash and boxes and rotting garbage. He lifted the man's body up and threw it onto the pile of debris. Charlie gave him back his gun. Fair was fair, right?

One more piece of garbage for the trash collector.

Problem solved.

He left The Magic Man—as well as the motel with its blood-stained carpet—behind him.

CHAPTER NINETEEN

Amy stretched, aware of the frailty of her own body. It startled her—as if pounds had melted from her bones overnight. Her thin arms reached toward the ceiling as her spindly fingers opened and closed in calisthenic gestures. It was Sunday. She rolled over on her side and closed her eyes to the morning light.

Another restless night. She found herself sleeping less and less in an attempt to prevent the dreams that haunted her. But the ones that happened during the day, when she was awake, were even harder to deal with. And far more difficult to rationalize.

As Amy turned her body, her feet kicked against something at the foot of the bed—something heavy that did not belong there. She pushed herself up with her elbows and opened her eyes, the dark shadows beneath them more pronounced than only a week ago. Her pixie features now bore the look of an old marsh crone peering through the grasses of a misty bog.

Amy's father stood across the room. On the foot of the bed sat a package topped with a big pink bow. Then she realized the significance of this day. Somehow, with all the events tumbling around her, it had completely slipped her mind.

"Happy birthday, Amy," Jerry said as he walked over and sat on the edge of his daughter's bed. "Go ahead and open it."

Her tiny fingers fought the ribbon and the paper until they fell away. She slid the cover from the box and peeled away the tissue that held her birthday surprise. "Oh Daddy, it's beautiful," she said as she lifted the dress from the box. The chiffon felt like a billowy cloud in her hands. "It's for a princess," she said.

"You are a princess. How would you like Sunday Brunch today at Le Chateau Bistro? Would that be nice enough for her highness?"

"Really, do you mean it? That's a fancy grown-up place. Really?"

"Really."

Amy hopped from the bed, dress in hand, and danced to the closet, ignoring the weakness in her legs.

"Daddy...," she said as she hung up the dress, "do you think Freddy could come too?"

"I've already asked him."

"Great!" she said. "And Daddy...those people keep saying they are helping me but I still can't make the dreams go away. They are getting more and more *worser*."

Again, Jerry felt helpless.

"It's going to take time," was all he could manage.

* * * * * * *

On Sunday afternoon Jerry Hamill, Amy, and Freddie sat at their table in Le Chateau Bistro. The tablecloth was white and on the table were two candles in porcelain candlesticks. The room was carpeted a bright kelly green and the walls were painted the same color beneath lacquered white latticework. It was like a summer garden, with potted ferns in greenhouse windows. A lone violinist strolled the room, dressed in a white tuxedo. His black moustache and curly hair gave him the appearance of an exotic spy in an old Peter Lorre film.

Amy looked pretty in her new dress. Her soft hair shone and her eyes, unable to mask her excitement, sparkled with delight. This place was special. Fun. It made her feel all grown up. Freddy sat to her left, fidgeting with the nautical brass buttons on his best blue blazer. He straightened his bow tie and cleared his throat. "This was really nice of you, Mr. Hamill." Then turning to Amy he said, "You should have gotten a double order of that pasta stuff, Amy. You are starting to look...kinda skinny."

Ignoring his remark, she turned to her father. "You've made today so special."

"I love you, angel," he said, knowing she must feel hurt that her mother had not called on her birthday. But she never called. The heartless bitch. Amy was tickled that Freddy had come and Jerry enjoyed the boy who spoke incessantly of computers and municipal bonds and his plans for the future . Freddy's fondness for Amy was obvious as he fussed over her. It was as if the boy chose each word with the sole purpose of building her self-esteem. He was insightful for a young boy. And kind. Amy was lucky to have found such a good friend.

They were two really great kids.

Reaching into his pants pocket, Freddy retrieved a small white box. He wiped the perspiration from his forehead using the sleeve of his blazer and pushed up the horn-rimmed glasses as they slid down the bridge of his nose. He handed the box to Amy. "Happy birthday," he said. "I picked it myself."

Amy took the box from Freddy and opened it. She held up the silver locket and smiled. It was shaped like a heart and etched on its front was a prancing unicorn. "It's beautiful," Amy said. "I will wear it forever." She leaned over and kissed his blushing cheek.

"Here, let me show you," he said, reaching for the locket. He pried it open with difficulty as his fingernails had long ago succumbed to his nervous habit of biting them to the quick. "See, there is a place for you to put two photos." He put the locket around Amy's neck, fumbling with the clasp until it held.

"Amy, you look beautiful," Jerry said. "Freddy, you could not have picked a more perfect gift."

"Yeah, it's really rad, huh."

"Rad?"

"You know, rad—bad. It's really bad," he said, puffing up with pride at his knowledge of a slang word used by the kids who were far more hip than he would ever be.

Amy's body shuddered—her eyes opened wide. "Bad," she

whispered, "Very bad." She stiffened in her chair, raising her hands to her throat. "Bad—bad man." The words came out in a whimper as she stood, knocking over the chair. Turning in a motion to run, she tripped and fell face first onto the carpet. She was all arms and legs as she scrambled to a sitting position.

Before Jerry could register what was happening, Freddy was on the floor beside Amy. He put his arms tightly around her and rocked her. "It's okay Amy—it's okay," he repeated. Jerry ran over to where they sat. The other restaurant patrons turned their attention to the disturbance.

"The bad man," she said. "He's coming...he's coming back again."

Jerry reached for his daughter.

"It's okay, Mr. Hamill, she'll be okay in a minute." Freddy continued holding her. "It happens lots at school—she'll be okay."

It happens lots? Jerry thought. What else didn't she tell him?

Jerry knelt on the floor next to the children.

"Oooh," Amy groaned, then screamed, "Help me! Help make it go away!" She choked and gasped, staring wide-eyed to a place far beyond them, then muttered the word, "Danger."

Jerry looked up. People at the surrounding tables were pointing and muttering. He lifted her into his arms. With a help-less motion of his arm, Freddy tried to cover his friend from the staring strangers.

"What the hell are you looking at?!" Jerry yelled across the room. "Just what the hell do you think you're staring at?!"

* * * * * * *

At that same moment, nearly forty miles away on a run-down street in Hollywood, Charlie Blackhawk knocked on a door. He held a large box wrapped in green paper. The package was topped with a perfect white satin bow. He felt exhilarated as he hummed a new rendition of The Birthday Song, swaying back and forth to his own melody, mumbling lyrics which held meaning to no one but himself.

The words that tumbled from his grinning mouth were vile, making his temples throb.

Charlie was invited to a birthday party.

He had never been to a real birthday party before.

He smiled as the door opened before him.

CHAPTER TWENTY

"Come on in," the fat lady said to Charlie Blackhawk. "Meg is expecting you." Betty held out her hand to him as Charlie stood motionless in the doorway. He looked at her fingers, short and plump as pasty links of uncooked pork sausage. He did not offer to shake her hand. "I'm Betty, Meg's roommate, and I don't bite," she laughed. "Now come on in, the party's inside."

Charlie stood on the front porch, trying to shake his frustration before stepping inside. He held Sabrina's birthday present tightly against his chest. He had thought only Meg and Sabrina would be there. He had come prepared, he reminded himself, as his right hand encircled the small bottle of chloroform in his jacket pocket. The jacket was new, a burgundy suede chosen just for this occasion. He bought it for a stranger, the man named Charles Black, the man that Meg and Sabrina could trust. He had to look the part—for now. It was just going to be happy birthday Sabrina, and then he would rescue her and make her safe. Fast and simple.

But the fat lady answered the door.

And voices came from inside.

And laughter.

Meg had not said there would be others. It should have been just the three of them. Why was she messing up everything?

He looked at Betty, a smile frozen across his rugged face. She repulsed him, reminded him of that giant banana slug in Oregon. It had been bigger than a Great Dane's turd and he could have sworn the thing raised its head and grinned at him.

He didn't like it one bit. He had covered it with dried leaves and set it on fire with his cigarette lighter. The ground had been damp, so it smoked and sizzled for a long time before he stomped out the smoldering leaves with his boot.

The fat lady wore a huge red caftan and the slug's smile, as if she knew what he had in his pocket—and what thoughts were swirling about inside his head. Like he was not really invisible at all. Charlie knew he would have to step easy. He walked past the sideshow freak and into the room. Meg entered, licking icing from her fingers, and introduced him to Betty and Jason Mittleman. Her sticky fingers pushed her hair from her face as she motioned Charlie to sit. The chair was in a corner, next to the TV, away from where Jason and Betty sat like Laurel and Hardy on the couch. This is real comic shit, he thought with a grin, trying his best to relax in this room full of strangers. Betty and Meg—and some faggot named Jason. It wasn't too bad...there were only three of them...but where was the girl they called Sabrina?

She was the reason he had come.

Charlie held the present on his lap as Jason broke the silence.

"I'm Meg's agent," he said. "Is she beautiful or what?"

"Agent? You mean Meg is a real live movie star? Wait until I tell the guys back home," he said in his best golly-gee, country boy voice. Practice makes perfect, he thought with pride.

Meg stood across the room and shrugged. Jason scowled at her lack of enthusiasm.

He heard Sabrina call her mother from in another room. When Meg returned, her daughter stood at her side. Sabrina's hair was pulled back with a blue ribbon that matched her dress and blue velvet slippers. The kind one finds in Chinatown, studded with tiny pearls and rhinestones. She stood nearly as tall as her mother and was every bit as beautiful. It was hard to believe this was a child of of twelve.

"Check out my shoes," she said. "Mrs. Cooney gave them to me for my birthday. She said she doesn't need fancies anymore—that is what she called them—fancies. Isn't that cute? Aren't they pretty?"

"Real nice," said Charlie. Second hand with fake pearls, he thought. I brought you something nice and new. When he handed her the package she thanked him, and placed it with the other gifts. Why couldn't she open it now? Nothing, absolutely nothing, was going as planned. Why wasn't she wearing the Girl Scout uniform? That was how he had rehearsed it. And her mother was the only one there and when she left the room he would take Sabrina and she would say, "I missed you, Charlie" and he would say, "I saved you."

That was how it was supposed to go—unless she didn't recognize him right away.

Then he would use the chloroform.

His exterior was calm as they all small-talked, but his insides shook like a jackhammer. Maybe he could just kill Meg and Betty and the faggot. It would be fun. But it might scare the girl. She might not understand it was right. He did not like having to come up with a Plan B. Especially at the last minute.

"Grubs on," said Betty.

Limp paper plates balanced on their laps while they laughed as if nothing was wrong.

"Cake?" Betty stood over him, balancing three plates. Had he missed singing happy birthday? Had he sung along? Had Sabrina already made her birthday wish? All he could remember was sitting there watching Meg swill champagne like there was no tomorrow, and wanting to tell her there well might not be. Not if he had his way.

"Grab one before they drop," she said, drawn into the intricacies of his face. She felt a chill. But Meg had been right about one thing. He looked like a handsome movie cowboy. Randolph Scott had a twinkle in his eye, but not Charles Black. For a split second a dark cloud passed over his face, blocking the sunny facade.

"Thank you, ma'am."

Betty turned from Charlie, toward the warmth of the room.

Sabrina had begun opening her gifts. They were piled in

front of her, except for one large package that sat on the floor by the TV. She unwrapped Charlie's forest green cardigan. "It's to match your Girl Scout uniform," he said. "For when you get cold." She thanked him and tossed it aside, then unwrapped a big, red suitcase from Betty. Meg and Betty exchanged glances when she asked when she would ever use it. Jason had given her videos. "Look," she said, "It's Rambo—and The Terminator!" Then Jason walked her to the big package on the floor and she opened a VCR. "This is the most fantastic birthday present ever," she said.

Charlie looked over at the crumpled green sweater that lay forgotten in its box.

Meg walked over to where her daughter sat on the floor and handed her a thick envelope. Sabrina opened it. "Tickets? Two airline tickets to Connecticut? For tomorrow?" She looked puzzled.

"How would you like to meet your grandmother?"

"I—you're really going to let me meet my grandmother?"

Meg handed her a slip of paper with a phone number on it. "Why don't you call her and tell her we're coming? She is expecting your call." Sabrina raced to the kitchen phone and dialed. The room was silent as she dialed the number.

Jason paced the room, then finally spoke to Meg. "This was supposed to be a surprise for you Meg, but you can't go tomorrow. You have an interview."

"Well, I can't go on an interview tomorrow."

"Read my lips, kid. You are one of only three that got a call back on that new series. It's practically yours."

Again, she showed no enthusiasm as she thought things over. "Okay," she finally said, "I'll change my flight to late afternoon and meet Sabrina there."

Charlie looked at Jason. Just look at him, he thought, with his high-powered phony bullshit. The little prick did not fool Charlie at all. Mr. Big Shot was nothing but one more stupid little shit. Charlie lit a smoke.

Sabrina's voice filtered from the kitchen. "Flight 70, and

then in St. Louis we get flight 318 into Hartford/Springfield; it arrives at 11:32 p.m. Yeah, I know that's kinda late. We could take a taxi...you will? I'm looking forward to meeting you too, Grandma—Grandmother.

Sabrina ran into the room. "Grandma will meet our flight!" she said, bursting at the seams.

"Betty, do you think...?" Meg began.

"Why don't you let me take her to the airport?" Charlie said.

"Thanks, but you're heading back to New Mexico tomorrow, remember?"

"I forgot. I guess I forgot." He shifted nervously in his chair. Time. There's still time. I've got all the time in the world, he thought. He leaned back in the chair, took a long drag from his smoke, and smiled to himself. He was setting his new plan in motion and for the first time that day he felt in control.

Meg poured herself another glass of bubbly.

Doesn't she ever get enough? Charlie wondered. A boozing slut is not a fit mother, even if she could hold her liquor. It dulls the senses, affects ones judgment,

IT KILLS CHILDREN!

"Congratulations on the interview, Meg," said Betty. "Now I can tell the world that I'm shacking up with a movie star. It will do wonders for my image. And yes, I will be happy to take Sabrina to the airport for you."

"But you work...."

"You call that work? Get serious. This is more important and it will give me an excuse to take the day off."

Charlie stubbed out his cigarette. Black gook had collected around the cigarette slots on the ashtray. It looked as if it had not been washed in a month. He set it on the floor beneath his chair and toyed with the zipper of his suede jacket as Meg, Betty and Jason continued in conversation. He was odd man out. He was The Invisible Man.

They hardly noticed he was there. Well, that was just fine and dandy.

Slowly, Charlie continued to zip and unzip the jacket as he

watched them.

All the time in the world, he thought.

Zip, unzip. Zip, unzip. Zip.

He stood up abruptly. "Thank you so much," he said. "They say city folks are cold, but you showed real hospitality to a total stranger and made me feel truly welcome. God will surely bless you for your kindness."

"Do you have to leave already?" said Meg, but she didn't really sound sorry at all.

"Time to go pack it up so I can hit the road early in the morning. Home awaits."

And he left.

CHAPTER TWENTY-ONE

"There was a lady doctor who touched me in bad places," Amy said. "But I liked the other lady. We talked. I was mad because I told Mrs. Petroff about the bad dreams and they took me away. But Ms. Flores said that sometimes grown-ups make mistakes but I could tell her things. She said I could visit her again."

It was Monday and today Amy got to miss school. "We're going to see her today," Jerry said.

"I am sorry I told Mrs. Petroff about the dreams, Daddy."

Jerry had been shocked when Ms. Flores had revealed their contents. Shocked and confused that his daughter could conjure such images. Disconcerted as to where Amy might have heard such things. "Don't worry about it, Amy," he said.

"But you were mad. I saw you. They thought bad things."

He tried to be honest with her. He told her that he had been furious, but had never been upset with her. "But the more I thought about it, the more I understood. Bad things sometimes happen to children, and if such actions can save one child from suffering, then it is worth it. This time they were wrong, but maybe next time they'll be right. Can you understand what I am trying to say?"

"There's horrible things in the world, aren't there, Daddy?"

"Yes, but there are good things, too. Like you."

Amy understood.

He hugged her and kissed her forehead. She closed her eyes and felt warm and loved and safe, and she knew that those feelings were some of the beautiful things of which her father spoke.

* * * * * * *

"We are not infallible," Ms. Flores said. "But I hope you understand that our initial avenue of investigation was justified."

Jerry looked at the psychologist. She was the first voice of sanity in this mess and he liked her. Her demeanor made him feel less confrontational.

"Amy feels abandoned—first by her birth mother and now by your wife," said Ms. Flores.

"And I feel helpless. Like I'm failing her."

"Mr. Hamill, in Amy's dreams the scenario always happens to someone else. This is so much like the classic personality split that many children develop as a means of dealing with abuse."

"She is not abused! You just said yourself that...."

"Just calm down. I agree with you. I believe you. But it leaves so many questions."

"If you believe me, then this legal charade should end now."

"It is more complex than that. Please be patient. I want to help Amy as much as you do, but it is going to take time."

"It has taken too long already."

Ms. Flores walked over to Jerry and put her hand on his shoulder as she spoke. "Mr. Hamill, progress is being made already, but it's not simple. I really feel that it is essential that Amy—and you—continue with these sessions."

"Legally, you are on thin ice. You and I both know that."

"Try to separate the issue of legality from our mutual desire to help her. Amy made an odd statement to me. She said, "Even when my mother was with us, something was missing. Like part of me was empty."

"What an odd statement," Jerry said.

"If we cooperate with each other, maybe we can figure things out."

* * * * * * *

Charlie Blackhawk grunted as he swerved the Sterling into the Van Nuys Flyaway lot. His guts were flip-flopping beneath his belt buckle. He had wiped the car clean, even the ashtray, and wore driving gloves so as not to leave fresh prints. He was invisible and intended to stay that way. It was time to get his Nova. His own car was as comfortable as an old easy chair.

Only today he had forgotten where he parked.

He finally spotted it and quickened his step, as he whistled a disjointed tune. He heaved a sigh as its familiar interior hugged him, welcomed him. He gunned the motor, pulled out of the space, and crawled toward the exit. He liked a motor he could hear. One that growled rather than purred. The old Nova strained and lurched, as if on some level even the corroding metal knew to fear him.

* * * * * * *

"When you get to the call back, will you see movie stars?" Sabrina asked Meg.

"You never know."

"You are so damned calm," Betty said. "I'd be pissing puppies."

"I guess I'm still in shock."

"But you deserve it all," Sabrina said to her mother. "You've earned it."

"Maybe I'm afraid to dream. The first time I did, I got kicked in the teeth."

"Well, just spit out those loose teeth and go on," said Betty. "Otherwise life just keeps on kicking."

"Yeah," said Sabrina, pushing away from the table. "I do like Chuck Norris—when life punches me in the gut, I just kick back." She did a karate kick, barely missing the stove. "Pow! Watch out for Roboscout!" Meg admired her kid's moxie. She knew when to kick back—hard. The kid had character and courage and good old-fashioned balls.

"She is right on," Betty said. "Introspection will rot your

brains, Meg. Just grab it and growl and don't analyze it to death. Sometimes life does hand us a gift."

* * * * * * *

Later that morning, Jerry Hamill took the stairs two steps at a time, knowing Amy would be busy with her catch-up assignments. But he was surprised to find that she was not in her room. He ran down the hall and stood in the doorway of his own bedroom. Amy sat at the dressing table, so engrossed that she didn't notice as he watched.

She looked grotesque.

She had painted her face with her mother's make-up. Bright blues and shocking pinks covered her delicate features like the paint of a ridiculous clown. There were tears in her eyes and the corners of her mouth frowned with determination.

"Amy?"

She looked up with a start. She reeked of familiar perfume and she had a knit shawl twirled around her neck.

"What are you doing, sweetie?" He asked.

"Do I look pretty yet?"

"You always look pretty."

"No, I'm ugly. Mommy even said so. But if I make myself pretty maybe she will come back."

It's Ms. Flores's fault, he thought, filling her head with psychobabble, putting emphasis where it did not belong.

"You are the prettiest girl God ever created. It was my fault your mother left, not yours."

"I heard what she said."

"People say things in anger that they don't mean—do not even think about it." But he knew the words haunted her. And he knew that placing blame was not the solution.

"I'm stupid and I'm ugly and you only say I'm pretty 'cuz you love me."

"That's what makes us pretty, Amy. Loving and being loved. So you see, you are overflowing with the kind of beauty that really counts."

"You mean like what God sees? People can't even see that!" Amy lifted the eyebrow pencil with determination and painted a thick line across her brow. She looked even more like a clown than before, like a French mime with a sad smile and a painted tear.

But Amy's tears were real.

"She will come back," Amy said stubbornly as she stared into the mirror. "If I can make myself pretty enough, she *will* come back."

* * * * * * *

Charlie Blackhawk held his head. It was as if atmospheric disturbances were short-circuiting his brain and it hurt. He felt lost, alone, abandoned. The desert sun touched the distant ridge, its reflection turning his face the color of an old penny. Motionless tumbleweeds hugged the desert floor like sleeping hedgehogs. He stood there, his body stiff and unyielding, his mind twisting.

First he blinked.

Next an arm twitched.

Then he bent his knee, kicked up clouds of sand with his boot, and shrieked like a scalded cat into the thick desert air. He was forgetting—and he was remembering. His mind spun out like a renegade asteroid.

God put mothers on this earth to teach kids their bible verses and to obey God's will. No need for school. No need for anyone beyond their four walls to know they existed. Momma would clutch her bottle and her bible and she would tell them so and when night fell she would find her own pleasures within those walls. And pretty soon she wanted more and she wanted him to play with Lucy Mae, too—and it was her fault he had made Lucy cry.

It was all her fault.

He needed to tell Lucy...he needed to know...he needed to—

what?

"What...?" Charlie whispered.

He had to hurry. He had a job to do. He had waited for this day, the most important day of his life. Today she would be rescued and everything would finally be right. This time there could be no complications. No screw ups. He could not let her down.

This time he had to save her.

He had the chloroform in his pocket, although he doubted he would need it. She would be happy to see him, but just in case... just in case she didn't know him, like last time—and the time before that. He got into the car and checked the paper bag on the seat. There was a small rag smeared with motor oil, duct tape, surgical gloves. His heart thumped in anticipation as he turned the key in the ignition. He lit a cigarette and the ash glowed menacingly as he inhaled, exciting him. He snickered, then began to hum, his mind dancing to a nursery rhyme. The melody was off-key and the lyrics were his own:

> "And if that lit-tle bird don't sing,
> Charlie'll tear off its fuck-ing wing,
> And if that lit-tle duck don't float,
> And if that...and if that...."

Nervous laughter escaped his throat, gurgling like a backed up septic tank.

He took a deep breath—gunned the motor—slid into reverse.

No more rehearsals.

It was time for the show to begin.

CHAPTER TWENTY-TWO

Sabrina Stinson shoved the clothes into her bright red suitcase and snapped the latches shut. She wondered why her mother hadn't told her sooner that she had a real grandmother. "Oh, Betty, I almost forgot!" she said as she ran to the living room. "I've gotta say goodbye to Miss Cooney."

Betty looked at her watch. "We're leaving in half an hour. There's no time."

"I'll run," she said as she flew out the door.

Sabrina sprinted up the street toward the Convalescent Home, making a quick stop at the liquor store for four Oh Henry®s to tide her friend over until she returned from her trip.

* * * * * * *

In Hidden Meadows, Amy and her father sat at the kitchen nook. She wasn't improving so he'd taken her to see the doctor. Unable to diagnose the cause of her fatigue, he'd sent them home with multi-vitamins, iron tablets that gave her a tummy ache, and pamphlets on proper nutrition. They sat at the table, sipping hot cocoa and watching birds play outside the window. Despite the sunshine, Amy felt restless, overcome by a sense of foreboding that wouldn't go away.

* * * * * * *

Betty paced uneasily as she waited for Sabrina to return.

They'd have to leave for the airport in ten minutes or she would never catch her flight and Sabrina still wasn't back. Betty sucked the perfumed center from a Twinkie, tore it open with her thumbs, and finished the job with her tongue. "Almost as good as sex, if memory serves me right," she said aloud. She looked at Meg's sketches on the fridge, then paced some more.

She thought she heard a car pull into the driveway. She walked across the room and looked out the side window.

* * * * * * *

Charlie Blackhawk steered the Nova up the driveway, coming to a halt behind an old Cutlass. The presence of the other car didn't alarm him. He figured it belonged to the slug. Betty, was that her name? Betty, Betty. Yes, that was it. He turned off the car, leaving the key in the ignition, and one at a time, with great difficulty, pulled on the tight surgical gloves. He felt in his pocket, reassuring himself the bottle was still there. Sometimes he forgot things, he knew, but not today. Today was important. He shoved the oily rag into the same pocket as the chloroform, then got out of the car and walked purposefully along the driveway and up the back steps.

He knocked on the door.

Waited.

The door opened. Betty stood there, confused. "Charles Black," she finally said. "I thought you'd gone back to New Mexico. I didn't recognize the car...."

"I came for the girl."

"You what ?" She bristled.

"Meg said I could take her to the airport. I came for the girl."

"You're not making sense," she said. She tried to slam the door, but his boot blocked her effort. He pushed hard, forced his way inside, shoved her bulky form against the kitchen wall. She was big but she was weak, out of shape, already panting. He easily blocked her fist as she tried to hit him.

"Where's the girl?"

"She's not here!"

"You're lying," he said, pushing Betty aside, and running frantically to check the other rooms. "Where is she? I know she's here."

Betty reached for the wall phone, her hands trembling, her heart in her throat. She picked up the receiver....

"...Has to be here," she heard him babbling from the other room....

...Began to dial, but her hands wouldn't stop shaking...mis-dialed, clicked frantically at the receiver, dialed again. Pain shot through her head as he hit her with something from behind. He tore the phone from her hand, slammed it back onto its cradle, threw her against the wall. Betty regained her balance and stomped her foot down, hard, onto Charlie's boot.

"Sumbitch!" he wailed and slapped her face, raising thick welts. "Where is she?"

"Crazy bastard!" Betty turned, opened the drawer, her hand searching frantically until she found it. She grabbed the butcher knife mid-blade, its sharp edge cutting into her flesh, drawing blood. God, the pain—

Spun around, knife in hand, to face her adversary.

"The girl!" he was yelling. His eyes were maniacal, unseeing. She lunged forward, found her mark, cut him.

She stepped back, realizing that she'd only grazed his shoulder. Her breathing was shallow, sporadic. Don't come back, Sabrina, she thought. Oh God, baby, please don't come back.

She had to protect Sabrina. She put up a brave but futile fight as Charlie grabbed her by the wrist and twisted.

Twisted.

Oh, the pain.

He squeezed until, unable to hold it tight any longer, she dropped the knife and it clattered to the floor. Charlie lunged for the knife. Betty turned to the kitchen door, grabbed the knob, tried to pull.

White hot needles of pain shot through her back, then

subsided, numbed. She turned, shocked, and stood face to face with Charlie. She raised both hands—slowly—as if they were moving through water, and aimed for his eyes. She'd scratch the crazy bastard's eyes out. Her arms rose up, slowly, so slowly. (Why wouldn't they move faster, she thought.)

"Slug," Charlie was chanting. "Slug, ugly old slug," and he was laughing and his eyes were still crazy and he was holding the bloody knife and.... (Where had the blood come from and why couldn't she move faster?)

Betty watched, as if through a soft-focus lens. The edges of her reality were gauzy, fuzzing over. He was raising the arm which held the knife—higher, higher. Slowly, her thumbs aimed for his eyes—had to make those crazy eyes go away. Don't come home, baby, don't...oh God, the knife, the knife....

...plunging deep into her chest. Then,

...the darkness.

Sabrina opened the front door. "I'm on time, see?" The room seemed oddly dark, felt empty. "Betty?" Then in a whisper: "Betty, are you there?" She shut the door softly behind her. "Betty?"

She saw his tall, ominous form step forward from the shadows. "I've come for you, Lucy Mae," he was saying. There was gentleness in the words, but his expression was frightening, sinister. A sense of dread snapped like the sharp teeth of a steel-jawed trap. He was coming toward her.

"Charles Black."

"Charlie, honey, remember? It's me—it's your Charlie." His arms were outstretched and as he moved closer and closer, tears welled in his eyes.

Gripped by fear, Sabrina ran toward the kitchen. "Betty," she said, but he grabbed her from behind, stopping her in her tracks. He held firmly as she struggled to escape. "She's not here, Lucy," he was saying, "I've come to take you home."

"I'm not Lucy, I'm Sabrina and I AM home. Now let go of me, you creep. Let go!" She continued to fight, frantically kicking backwards at the man who held her. He spun her around so that she faced him, never loosening his hold.

"Don't be afraid," he said. His expression was confused, bewildered. "Something's not right. You're supposed to be happy now. I came to make you safe."

"Let go of me, you fucking creep!"

"I know what it is," he said calmly. "I know what's wrong." He held her by one arm and dragged her to the bedroom. She fought hard, grabbing futilely at the doorjamb as he shoved her through the door, but he pried her fingers loose, then he lifted her and threw her onto the bed.

Sabrina froze. He's going to rape me, she thought. Rape me and kill me and oh God, he wasn't after Meg, he was after me... and he's going to rape me. Too big—too strong—but I have to fight him, somehow outsmart him, fight him....

"You have to change your clothes now," he was saying, "so we can go."

"What?" It was all so frightening, so confusing, so...crazy.

"Put on your Girl Scout uniform and the pretty green sweater and then everything will be okay and then we can go."

Slowly, cautiously, Sabrina rose from the bed. "You're right..., Charlie," she whispered. "I have to change now so we can go."

His shoulders relaxed, relieved that she finally understood. "The uniform," he repeated.

"Yes, Charlie, I have to put on the uniform." Her heart pounded. He just stood there looking at her, not moving. "You have to leave the room now, Charlie."

"I can't leave you, Lucy." Then, tentatively, "You're trying to trick me, aren't you?"

"No Charlie, I want to go with you, really I do, but I can't change in front of you. You can understand that, can't you?"

His eyes darted nervously around the room. "I can't do that. You might trick me."

"You have to go so I can change."

He looked at her with suspicion. "All right, but I'm right outside the door, so don't try any funny stuff."

"I won't Charlie, I promise."

The door shut. Sabrina was alone. What am I going to do? She thought. Calm down, first you have to calm down. Be cool. She crossed the room to the open closet, pulled the uniform from its hanger and threw it onto the bed. She opened a drawer and tossed over her sweater. Just be cool. Sitting on the edge of the bed, she loosened the velcro straps on her shoes and pulled them off. They hit the floor with a thud.

The door flew open.

"What's going on?" Charlie asked.

"Damn it, I told you I need my privacy!"

"I thought...."

"Well you thought wrong," she snapped, "so get out of here." She regretted having yelled at him, anything could set him off, she was certain of that—but he had startled her. She held her breath, waiting for the consequences.

"I'm sorry, Lucy Mae," he said with a sheepish grin as he walked out and shut the door. She thought she heard sobs, then giggles from the other room. Oh shit, he's stark-raving, crazy mad, she thought. Crazy as a bedbug, that's what old Miss Cooney would say, crazy as a bedbug. I've got to get out of this—somehow—what would Bronson do? Or Rambo...or Chuck Norris? She was frantic. She couldn't think straight. She removed her clothing with trembling hands and slipped into the uniform and sweater, then remembered—something.

It wasn't much, but it was something.

She rifled through the sock drawer, took out her Girl Scout knife, slipped it into her pocket. Not much of a weapon—no machete or Uzi or even a reliable old Luger, but it was something and that was better than nothing at all. She put on the Chinese slippers over thick, orange socks. For luck. They were from her friend and they'd bring her luck, wouldn't they? Luck, she repeated in her mind. That was crazy, crazy as a bedbug, crazy like Charlie. And where were Betty, Meg, and Buddy when she needed them? Her thoughts were racing—anxious, senseless, disconnected.

"Hurry up," the voice said from outside the door.

"I'll be right there," she answered. "Stop rushing me!"

And then, from outside the window, she saw old Mr. Owens shuffling slowly down the driveway which separated their two houses, stringy hair falling forward from his bowed head. She ran to the window—tried to open it. It was stuck. "Mr. Owens," she yelled, banging her fists against the cracked pane. "Mr. Owens!" But the old man did not look up. "Oh shit, for once in your life turn up your hearing aid. Mr. Owens, help me!" She continued pounding on the glass. Maybe if she could shatter it he would hear her...tears of frustration burned her eyes.

The door flew open with a crash.

Sabrina turned.

Charlie stood in the doorway, enraged. "You tried to trick me," he said, lunging toward her.

"Don't touch me, you dirty cretin." she said, dodging him. What WOULD Chuck Norris do? Charlie grabbed at her again, this time barely missing his mark. As hard as she could, with every bit of strength she could muster, Sabrina let loose with a sideways kick. "ROBOSCOUT!" she yelled, "Don't mess with Roboscout!" and her foot found its target, landing heel-first into Charlie's groin with a hard thud. She smiled triumphantly as she heard him gasp, then scrambled to the door, turning to look back. He was grinning at her, like he'd enjoyed it, like she'd just given him a winning lottery ticket or something.

Sabrina ran toward the front door, tripped, regained her footing, and reached the door. If she could just get outside she could run for help. But he grabbed her from behind and held her in a chokehold, was holding some sort of cloth over her face.

"Nobody fucks with Charlie Blackhawk," he said.

The cloth felt rough against her skin and it stunk.

"It's okay, we're going home now," he said.

She felt light-headed. Gas stations—all she could think of were gas stations. Gas stations.

She saw row after row of gas stations as far as the eye could see....

Then everything turned black.

* * * * * * *

Amy Hamill bolted upright from where she sat at the nook in her kitchen and looked out the window. "Owns, owns, owns," she chanted, hitting the glass with her fists, frightening away the birds. She turned and stared at her father, then ran to the center of the kitchen, turned and looked at him again.

"Dirty croutons!" she screamed at her father. "Croutons, croutons, cretins, cretins, cretins." Then she wrinkled her nose, as if smelling something terrible, and, before her father could reach her she collapsed and fell to the floor.

* * * * * * *

Five blocks from Sabrina's house, Charlie pulled the old Nova into an alley and changed back the license plates. He then drove up the Santa Monica Boulevard on-ramp onto the Hollywood freeway and headed toward downtown Los Angeles. He turned, looking into the back seat where the girl slept under a blanket. She was breathing. That was good. At the interchange he picked up the San Bernardino Freeway and headed toward the distant mountains.

In less than two hours he'd be in Pine Lake.

CHAPTER TWENTY-THREE

There were no customers in the General Store, so Jan Smith turned up the radio. Heavy Metal blasted at eardrum-splitting decibels as she danced wildly across the floor, stomping her feet angrily on the floor boards, her yells echoing and bouncing off the walls and down the empty aisles. Printed across the front of her black t-shirt was Ozzie Osborne—The No More Tours Tour. She was bored. This place is lobotomized, she thought. It sucks. She dreamed of a faceless city devoid of prying eyes. A place where she'd be free to boogie—or pierce her nose—or spray her hair purple if she wanted.

Distant lightning illuminated the afternoon sky. Cumulonimbus clouds scudded across the heavens, threatening rain—or worse. A tumultuous flash bolted across the darkening sky. Then another. And another. Good show, Jan thought as she turned off the music. She listened as the sound of far-off thunder drum-rolled across the sky, then another—closer—until finally she felt the floor shudder beneath her feet. "Fuckin' A!!!" she yelled. The storm cracked, sizzled, vibrated. Jan was impressed. It was like having a front row seat at a Zeppelin concert. Maybe even better. She tugged at her short black hair, trying to lift the spikes. The lights flickered, hesitated. She shook her head wildly, then danced and stomped across the room like a frisky colt to the rhythmic drumbeat of the thunderstorm.

Bright electrical flares flashed across the blackening sky.

She stopped dancing and watched the rain pelt against the window, and when the lightning flashed again, it illuminated the outline of the beat up Chevy Nova as it turned up the old dirt road.

Things were starting to look up.

HAWK was back.

* * * * * * *

Sabrina Stinson was dreaming. Nonsensical, disconnected pictures on a torn movie screen. There were gas stations, hundreds of them, and they were crawling with bedbugs. Vile, wiggling things clung to the structures and spilled onto the blacktop. They held tightly to the gas pumps like dark, breathing tendrils of ivy. And there was the aroma of pine beneath the stench of gasoline. Suddenly Buddy was there, her make-believe friend, holding a bottle of Pine-Sol® in one tiny hand and a coarse rag in the other. She began to scrub away the bugs—and they crawled up her arms and onto her face, but she kept on scrubbing. There were sounds like cannon blasts or Uzi fire, but as the images faded, the effluvium of gasoline and Pine-Sol® lingered.

Sabrina's head ached. It was difficult to breathe through her nose but her mouth was covered. With what? The atmosphere felt cold and damp and foreboding. Where was she? Her body ached even worse than her head as she tried to turn onto her side but found she could not move.

Something was holding her.

She was bound with ropes.

She opened her eyes to a room that was small and musty and dark.

She heard wind and rain and thunder.

On the opposite wall from where she lay, there was a small window. Outside the window stood a tall pine, its branches creaking in prophetic moans against the wind—as if they knew that death—or something worse—lay in wait. Yellow-white bolts stabbed downward, their light flickering across the room.

Then she saw him.

He was standing next to a fireplace. Watching her.

It was Charlie.

(Nobody fucks with Charlie Blackhawk, he'd said.)

She remembered.

She fought desperately against her restraints as his tall, dark form walked over to where she lay. He leaned down, exhaling his sour breath. She tried to turn away. The ropes abraded her skin as she fought them. Savage pain shot through her every nerve. She tried to scream but couldn't. She turned her face to the window, preferring the thunderous storm to the terror who hovered over her.

"I'll remove the tape," he was saying. "You can scream if you want, but nobody can hear you. There ain't nobody here for miles except for you and me."

She turned and looked into his eyes. She knew that no one would hear her screams—and she knew that Charlie Blackhawk had taken her to the edge of a dark world where no one dwelled but the two of them.

"You promise to be good now," he said, ripping the silver duct tape from her mouth. It stung like blazes but she refused to react.

She took a deep breath.

"Cretin!"

He reacted as if she had slapped him—hard, but he said nothing.

"When my father finds us you'll be dead meat," she threatened, unable to come up with anything better to say.

"You have no father, Lucy Mae. No father and no mother—you only have your Charlie, and he'll take good care of you."

"I don't want you to take care of me. I want to go home." She pulled at her restraints, then spit on him, spraying his face with her saliva. Slowly, Charlie raised his hand to his face, wiping off her spittle...then put his hand in his mouth. He sucked the saliva from his fingers and smiled at her. He wasn't at all like the quiet, polite cowboy from out of town that her mother had invited to her birthday party. Meggie had asked him to their home out of kindness, but it was as if this stranger had turned into some-body else. Someone evil. He was creepy, nuts...deranged.

Sabrina sensed that defiance would be useless against her captor. This time she wasn't just mouthing off to the Magic Man on the safety of a busy Hollywood street corner—it was easy to be brave there. She was facing a madman on his own turf and didn't even know where that was. Or how far away she was from the safety of her home. *Or what he wanted with her.* They were sequestered in a dark corner of nowhere and they were the last two people on earth.

Outside the storm raged.

Sabrina had never considered the idea that twelve-year-old girls could die. Not like this. Not until now. A child's innocent fantasy sees the world as a forever kind of place and they see themselves as indestructible. But they can fall out of trees or get cancer or get hit by cars—or cross paths with the likes of Charlie Blackhawk. Sabrina's heart pounded as she realized that, before this nightmare could end, one of them would have to die. Either Roboscout or the bedbug. It was just a matter of odds—and those odds weighed heavily in Charlie's favor. He was huge and he was strong. Much stronger than she could ever be. And he also had the advantage of knowing where he was—and what his plans were. It wasn't much of a contest and she was scared.

Buddy, she thought.

"Will you be a good girl now?" Charlie asked.

"Yes, Charlie," she answered. "I'll be a good girl now."

The rain pecked out a solemn eulogy against the window.

* * * * * * *

The dream awoke Amy Hamill. She was surprised to be in her own bed. Daddy must have put her there but she did not remember. The room was dark. As she slipped from the bed, she noticed that she was still in her play clothes.

Amy left her bedroom and went downstairs.

Her father was in the study, going over legal documents. Amy stood in the doorway. Jerry smiled tenderly at his daughter. "Come over here," he said, setting his work aside. She walked over to him and climbed up onto the safety of his lap. She hoped that his hugs would erase the nightmare, but they didn't.

"The bad man has her and it's dark and there are bugs."

"It was only a dream."

An overpowering sadness slipped through Amy. She relaxed her arms, allowing them to fall onto her lap.

"Yes, " she said. "It was only a dream."

Jerry looked down at his daughter. It was then that he saw the welts on her wrists. He lifted her hands, turned them over. "What are these marks?" he asked.

Amy looked at them, bewildered.

"It was only a dream," she repeated.

CHAPTER TWENTY-FOUR

It was well after midnight when Meg Stinson pulled into her driveway. She had tried to change her flight to that night, but was unable to get one until tomorrow. She had tried to call Betty several times earlier in the evening, but there had been no answer. Betty must have hit a movie or something after taking Sabrina to the airport. Meg had wanted Betty to join her at a little jazz club on Ventura Boulevard. It would have been more fun in the company of her best friend. After four futile phone calls trying to reach her, she gave up. The music was good and so were the drinks and her sense of time just got away from her.

The sky was dark with no stars. There rarely were in the city, for a million temporal lights extinguished them. Meg thought about Connecticut. She remembered the night sky that belonged to her as a girl, shimmering jewels tossed recklessly across a black velvet backdrop, glittering white, silver, blue, red—each one a distant sun in a faraway universe, reminding her that she was no more than a speck, but a miracle all the same. Tomorrow she would fly back to her yesterday—to see the sky and inhale the fresh air. And to share it all with Sabrina. She would reunite with her past and try to erase the worst of the interim years. Could there ever be forgiveness without apologies? Betty had said never to apologize.

Meg turned off the engine. The house was unlit. Betty's car was there and she always left a light on but just this once she must have forgotten. Meg walked to the door and heard the telephone ringing, ringing, ringing. She ran into the house, through the darkness and into the kitchen. She fumbled blindly for the phone and picked up the receiver.

"Hello?"

"You should have told me that you changed your plans."

"Mother? Is that you?"

"I've been waiting here at the airport for hours. This is just too inconvenient, Mary Margaret. The plane arrived on time and she wasn't on it. You should have told me."

"Of course she was on the plane," Meg said. "You just didn't recognize her. Have her paged...."

"I did. Several times."

"This doesn't make any...." As Meg shifted her weight her foot slid out from under her. She fell to the floor with a painful thud, the receiver dropping as she fell. "Oh shit!" she said, fumbling for the cord.

"Mary Margaret, are you there?" Her mother's voice bubbled, as though surfacing through deep water.

Meg leaned on one hand, pushed up from the floor, regained her balance, then slipped again. "Shit," she repeated. The floor felt wet and sticky. Betty or Sabrina had spilled something and had neglected to clean up the mess. What the hell was it? Ketchup? Pancake syrup? She tried again to regain her footing, pulled herself up—

"Mary Margaret?"

—fumbled through the darkness for the telephone cord, found it—

"Are you there?" Her mother's voice cracked through the wires.

—reeled in the cord, clutched the receiver, held the phone to her ear.

"I'm sorry, mother. Are you still there? I fell. It's dark in here. Sabrina was on the flight, you must have just...."

"I'm telling you that she was not!"

"Hold on a minute so I can turn on the light. Maybe you'll make more sense if I turn on the light." The flat of Meg's hand swept along the smooth surface of the wall, searching for the switch. She found it, clicked it on. Light blazed through the room like a flare. Meg blinked—focused—saw Betty on the floor. Just sitting there. Staring at nothing.

The knife,

and the *blood!*

And her own bloodied hand clutching the phone. She dropped it. The receiver swung on the end of the cord, knocking against the wall in a frantic heartbeat. Meg ran through the house, turning on lights, searching for her daughter.

Meg screamed Sabrina's name, over and over.

The house was empty.

Dead.

She raced back to the kitchen—the phone—incomprehensible, confused words.

She hung up and dialed 911. More disconnected phrases. Hung up.

The phone rang again.

* * * * * *

The telephone was still ringing when the police arrived. They found Meg sitting on the kitchen floor. Her head was tilted to one side, nestled against the dead woman's breast, her hair matted with blood. She was holding her friend, comforting her, and gently and sweetly rocking her in her arms.

CHAPTER TWENTY-FIVE

Daybreak had arrived with a cover of mammoth clouds that soon dissipated. Blue jays scolded the new day. Liquid sunshine stained the sky, filtering through the copse of pines outside the cabin.

But here the sunlight held no promise.

Charlie Blackhawk stood in the cabin's kitchen, coiled in frustration, cursing as he surveyed the food supply. The cheese was molding. The bread was stale. He had forgotten to pay the utilities. He opened the kitchen door and hurled the loaf outside. Birds squawked and scattered, their wings beating a frantic retreat upward to the safety of the sky. He slammed the door.

Charlie stood, staring at the food, then began humming. Nothing would ruin this day. He was fixing his little sister her 'welcome home' breakfast and he was happy. He removed a dirty steak knife from the sink, wiped the blade across his jeans, then dug mold spots from the cheese, absent-mindedly popping the green pieces into his mouth and eating them. He placed a handful of crackers on a plate, topping them with perfectly cubed cheese squares. He smiled, proud of his handy work—Lucy Mae would be pleased.

Sabrina had slept fitfully. Despite the lit fireplace, the night was cold. Her bones ached. Her lower back ached. Sleep came hard with bound wrists and ankles. It had been impossible to relax while Charlie Blackhawk paced in the darkness. The storm had passed sometime during the night, but the blackness remained—the dark, evil presence of the man who had brought her here. She looked around the room and the room was her prison. She made a mental note of every detail...the stone fireplace, the window to its left, the pine branch scraping mournfully against the dirty window pane. Mottled patches of sunlight clung to the walls. An old Girl Scout calendar hung on the wall held by a rusty nail. The girl in the calendar photo had Sabrina's red hair but she stood in the sunshine, free and smiling. Sabrina was not free nor was she smiling. She was being held hostage in an unknown prison. On her left was a heavy door and another small window to the left of that, its view smothered by carelessly tacked newspapers, brittle with time. What secrets was he hiding here that he felt the need to block the window? He had said there was no one for miles. What was he afraid of? Could he really be afraid of anything? She doubted it.

Sabrina lowered her eyes to the bare and worn wood floor. To the right of the fireplace was the straight-backed chair where Charlie had sat, and beyond that she could see into a cramped kitchen. The room where Sabrina lay smelled of dust and dirt and decomposition. There was little furniture in the room, just the basics. A chair, the sofa bed, an end table and a dresser. To her right was a narrow door, which she hoped led to a bathroom.

She had to pee and she had to escape.

Charlie entered the room and walked over to Sabrina. With a prideful grin he pushed the plate toward her, waiting for his praise. She turned away. "You have to eat," he said. "I made it special for you."

"I have to pee, that's what I have to do."

He stood over her, confused. He looked at the plate, then at the bathroom door, then at the ropes which bound her. He blinked.

"You'll try to trick me again."

"Damn it, I've got to go to the bathroom!"

He sat down the plate on the end table and walked over to the bathroom. He opened the door and studied the tiny room. The small window above the toilet was not large enough for her to fit through. She couldn't escape from there. There was a shower stall. He removed the packet of razor blades from the shelf above the sink and put them in his pocket.

Sabrina watched from where she lay bound on the sofa bed.

"I can't let you go in there," he said. "Not alone, I can't."

"What do you think I'm going to do, turn into a mouse to get through that dinky window? Get real."

"Not alone," he repeated.

"Like hell, not alone! Now untie me before I have an accident."

"Little girls ain't supposed to cuss," he said, then walked back to the bathroom. He grabbed the small hook on the door molding and twisted until it broke free from the wood. He put it in his pocket, shut the door, then reopened it, looking again at the tiny window.

Charlie walked over to the sofa bed and untied Sabrina's ankles, then her wrists. "No funny stuff," he kept repeating as he untied her. She rubbed her reddened skin in an effort to ease the pain. She rose to a sitting position and turned, letting her feet touch the floor. She walked the short distance to the bathroom and closed the door.

Sitting on the toilet, she studied the room. The window was too small. She pulled up her panties and smoothed her uniform, then stood on the toilet seat to see outside. There was nothing in her line of vision but trees—giant evergreens, western Juniper, Ponderosa pine. She could see no cabins or houses or even a road. Just trees and mountains. Where was she?

She stepped down, flushed the toilet, opened the door. Charlie was standing on the other side, listening and waiting. How gross, she thought. Had he been listening to her pee? How sick is that? She brushed past him and sat on the bed.

"Okay? You happy now?"

"I didn't want to lose you."

"Well, big whooping surprise! I'm still here."

"I made this for you," he said, handing her the plate. Sabrina wanted to refuse it but she was famished. She'd eat, because she was hungry, but she'd be damned if she'd enjoy it—or thank him. She ate in silence as Charlie watched her and waited for her to voice her approval. He was disappointed that it didn't come.

"I'm thirsty," she finally said, breaking the silence.

He went to the kitchen, never letting her out of his sight, and returned with an empty glass and a can of Budweiser. He apologized that there was nothing else to drink. (Tap water hadn't entered his mind.) He pulled the tab and poured half into a glass for Sabrina. She raised the glass to her lips. It tasted warm and bitter. While she drank, he chugged down the rest from the can.

She wondered why adults drank that stuff. It tasted nasty and just half a glass had made her feel light-headed.

"I have to tie you up now," he said.

"The ropes hurt me."

"I'm sorry, Lucy Mae." (What was all this Lucy Mae shit? she thought.) "But I have to...until you remember." He rebound her ankles and wrists. She tried to identify what knots he was using, but he moved too fast. If she could figure out the knots, just maybe, she could untie them. But once again she was bound and helpless. Now he's going to rape me, she thought. Feed me, then rape me, then kill me. It was the only thing that made any kind of sense.

Instead, Charlie went over to the chair and sat. She sighed. But it's just a matter of time, she told herself. Her captor stared at her with chilling intensity as her mind reeled.

"Are you holding me for ransom? My mother doesn't have any money. We've got *less* than no money. You saw our house!"

But he was silent.

Think Sabrina, she told herself. Think!

But the beer had made her groggy and she closed her eyes.

* * * * * * *

When Sabrina woke up she felt something on her leg. Opening her eyes, she saw that Charlie had hoisted her Girl Scout dress up around her hips and was running his hand along her thigh.

She screamed as she threw her body away from him.

"Don't touch me you creepy perv!"

"Gotta. Momma says I gotta, Lucy, Momma says."

Sabrina sobbed as she squirmed, in an attempt to escape his searching hands. He abruptly stopped, stood up and began pacing the room, screaming: "Can't make me Momma, no, she's my Lucy! (So that was it, Sabrina thought as she watched in disbelief.) Can't make me, please don't make me, I don't wanna make Lucy cry. I don't want her to go away again. No, Momma!" Then in a taunting, feminine voice: "If thy hand offend thee, Charlie, if thy hand offend thee." He yelled at his demon, "Not this time, no!" Back and forth he paced, laughing, crying, pacing, laughing. Finally, he sat down, head in hands, shoulders drooped.

The room had gone from pandemonium to the stillness of a morgue. Sabrina watched, unsure if he was breathing—afraid to breathe herself.

"Charlie?"

His eyes were glazed as he looked up.

"Charlie, I'm your sister, right?"

"Of course you are, you know that."

"And I came back, right?"

He nodded.

"Where have I been?"

"Dead."

The calmness of his tone sent shivers up her spine. He'd killed his own sister, she thought, and now he's going to kill me.

"But you came back," he smiled, "and now everything is going to be okay."

"And Momma, Charlie, where's Momma?"

"Momma was bad and Momma let you die." His lip quivered.

Sabrina knew that to survive, she'd damn well better *BE* this Lucy Mae. She had no choice. She had to buy time. Roboscout in disguise. Yeah, she could do that. This was a maniacal game created by a madman and she didn't know the rules. But she was good at games.

"But now I'm back," she said.

"I missed you, Lucy."

Were those tears in his eyes? she wondered. Was this monster really capable of crying?

"I missed you too, Charlie." Her pulse was throbbing in her ears. She wanted to be sick. She had a headache and her back still hurt.

She needed Buddy.

She said a prayer, begging God to save her from the madman.

* * * * * * *

In Hidden Meadows, Amy Hamill knelt on the floor beside her bed. She was still wearing her flannel nightie and smelled of Ivory Soap. Her hands were clasped together, her head bowed.

"...I pray the Lord my soul to take...." She stopped, shuddered. "The madman," she said, "and save me from the madman. Amen."

Her father stood in the doorway, listening to his daughter's midday prayer. He looked in puzzlement at the marks on her wrists, and the fresh abrasions on her ankles.

Jerry Hamill's heart was pounding.

* * * * * * *

Charlie Blackhawk sat in the cabin's darkness, listening to the voices that played like a never ending tape inside his head. The voices that told him what to do. The voices that haunted him.

"But Momma, Lucy's still sick."

("Ain't nothin' but a cold.")

"But Momma!"

("Stop yer naggin' on me!")

"But she needs a doctor, Momma. My Lucy is all rattley like."

("Don't you dare question your Momma." She took a drink from the whiskey bottle as she glared at her son. "She'll be just

fine. You wanna take her to a doctor so's he can see you been messin' with her? Is that what you want Mr. Smarty-pants?")

"No, Momma."

"Don't gotta listen!"

Charlie's words echoed through the cabin.

* * * * * * *

Jason Mittleman stood in the center of the living room flailing his arms and pacing. "You have to snap out of it," he said to Meg.

"My best friend was murdered and my daughter is missing and you're fucking telling me to snap out of it?"

"I'm only trying to help. I loved Sabrina too." He pulled the bottle of champagne from her grip and threw it across the room adding it to the empty bottles strewn around the floor. This was a side of her he hadn't seen before. He sure as hell didn't need some drunk showing up on interviews slurring her words and blowing his potential commissions.

"Loved? *Loved*?! You sound like you already have her dead and buried. She's alive and I'm going to be right here when she comes back."

"You've probably got the part. Focus on that. There's nothing you can do..."

"I have to be here in case the phone rings and it's Sabrina!"

Jason said nothing.

"My daughter is missing. Why? And Betty is dead. Who could have done that to her? Why? Why? *Why?* She was such a wonderful person. And they zipped her up in a body-bag, Jason. Then they carried her out of here like she was nothing but yesterday's garbage. She was my best friend, for God's sake! They didn't even...I had to clean up the blood. I had to wash my *best friend* from the kitchen floor—and the walls. Do you have any idea what that was like? I scrubbed and scrubbed...."

"I'm sorry," was all he could think to say.

"Then I spent the rest of the night making a flyer. With

Sabrina's photo. Maybe somebody saw something. Maybe they will call me. First thing this morning I took it to the newspaper and convinced them to insert it into tomorrow's edition. It cost me every dime I have and I don't care. The police are too damn slow and minutes count."

"Why not just let the cops do their job?"

"I don't trust them to do their job!"

"At least let me do mine."

"You'd make a lousy fucking actor, Jason. You wouldn't make a cent off of yourself. Insincerity reeks from your every pore. Money, that's all you care about. I'm your ticket to your ten percent. You're as bad as the rest of them in this shithole town. You know what, Jason? Pretty blondes are common as dirt in Hollywood—why don't you just go and find another one? Fuck you. Fuck this business. Fuck it all. I'm done!"

CHAPTER TWENTY-SIX

Sabrina walked into the kitchen, shoulders drooping like an old woman, her pretty blue Chinese slippers shuffling across the floor. The slippers had come to symbolize her other world. It was important to remember that other place. Betty, Buddy, her mother, Miss Cooney. Even the Magic Man was better than this. But they were far away and unreal—except for Buddy. In this forsaken place, Buddy was the only one who seemed real. Make-believe Buddy. Nonsense, she told herself, I'm getting as bugshit as Charlie.

She felt weary as she stood at the sink and looked out the window. A cloud drifted past the sun, cutting the light to a haze as gray as Charlie's eyes. He followed her into the room and sat down. At least he trusted her more now. He would untie her, but he never stop watching. His shadow clung to her like a death shroud. She felt as if she was in a dark well trying to grab hold of the light, to pull herself from the darkness.

Her uniform stunk. She hadn't showered. She was afraid to.

There was no lock.

And the kitchen smelled.

"We need food," she said. It didn't bother him—he rarely ate. He just drank beer and lost track of time. So did she. It was all blurred, like the time she'd gone to the Chuck Norris film festival and tried to watch five movies in a row. Charlie made her feel like that as he replayed the same scenario over and over again. It paralyzed her. It was strange, as if he needed to rehearse something again and again until he got it right. Got what right? He would touch her, pull away, laugh, cry, scream, argue with Momma (that was the worst of all), until he'd slip into his catatonia.

He needed her to be Lucy Mae, she knew that much. But she could not imagine that in some small corner of his jumbled brain he didn't know the truth. She'd pretend until she almost believed it herself. It was important. He needed some kind of validation from her, but her instincts told her that as long as she withheld her approval the game would go on and she'd be safe. It was a strange game and she hoped she was playing it right.

"It smells awful in here. Don't you ever clean up?" She stood at the counter, looking for something edible. A cardboard carton sat on the countertop. Chinese food, she thought, not caring how old it might be. She removed the lid. Nightcrawlers squirmed in dark mulch. How disgusting, she thought, shaking the carton and watching them wiggle. Worms. Why worms?

"Charlie," she asked sweetly, "are we by water?"

No answer.

"Are we by a lake?"

"'Member when we used to creek fish?"

"Sure. It was fun, wasn't it Charlie? Can we do it again?"

He looked at her with suspicion. "Are you tricking me?"

(*Nobody fucks with Charlie Blackhawk.*)

"I just want to be outside sometimes. And I'd really like us to go fishing...like we used to."

"I'll think on it."

You're a smart one Charlie Blackhawk, she thought, but I'm smarter.

She turned to the window and spotted the Mason jar sitting on the counter and picked it up. It appeared to be stuffed with tissue. She unscrewed the lid and the stench of decomposition escaped. She saw long teeth protruding from a tiny mouth frozen in a scream, and empty sockets sunken into matted fur. The jar crashed into the sink and shattered. She vomited onto the jar and onto the dead rat-thing. Every time she gasped for breath she inhaled the death smell and vomited again. She vomited until there was nothing left in her but dry heaves. She'd under-estimated him. Charlie enjoyed killing things.

He followed her back to the bed, bound her, then sat in the chair staring at the wall.

Sabrina could be Sabrina now.

She tugged at the ropes but they were unyielding . If I could figure out the knots, she thought. Knots, what was it about knots that kept gnawing at her? Then she remembered. She'd been concentrating on knots on one of the nights she'd floated above her body. That had happened to her twice now. Focusing on knots and badges and more knots. That had been the beginning. I'll do it again, she told herself. She concentrated with all her might but nothing happened. Breathe deep. Relax. It was hard with Charlie across the room. But that's why she had to. Think of knots. And Buddy. And home. Finally she felt her body tingle as if a million butterfly wings were caressing her, then she quiv-ered. She felt as if she were floating high in the clouds. She opened her eyes and realized she was hovering near the ceiling. She looked down upon her own form where it rested on the mattress—and at Charlie Blackhawk as he stared through the emptiness.

It scared her, but there was no time for fear. She had to act. The other time she had wished herself into Betty's room. This time she thought of freedom and in that same instant found herself outside the cabin. Her ethereal self hovered in one spot, like a hummingbird unsure of which way to fly. She was free, floating above the tall Ponderosa pine, pregnant with fist-sized cones, and more trees, and fallen logs that lay like severed limbs upon the ground. She ascended higher, looking for clues as to her location—and wondered if she could escape like this. Just float away—or would her other body die back inside the cabin—leaving her drifting for eternity? Was this what death was like? If so, wasn't it better than dying at the hands of Charlie Blackhawk? The choice was easy. She soared upward, toward the light and away from the darkness.

Then—thud.

She was back in the cabin, tied hand and foot, lying in the bed.

"If thy hand offend thee!" He screamed. He was standing by the fireplace as he reached into his pocket and pulled out a small object. He laughed as he unwrapped it, then held it above his head, his arm stretched high, as though making an offering to his demon god.

He was grinning.

A spark of sunlight glinted across the object. It was a razor blade.

Sabrina held her breath, knowing she was about to die.

"If thy hand...." Charlie laughed. His upheld arm plunged downward in a swift, slashing motion, slicing through the back of his other hand, again and again and again and he laughed and he cried and he kept repeating, "If thy hand, if thy hand, if thy hand," in his nightmarish chant.

"Stop!" Sabrina yelled, but he didn't hear her. He was in his other world.

"Look Momma, it's time for the watching games!" Again the razor found its mark. "See? See? See?"

"Stop Charlie, stop it! Momma's not here, Charlie stop." She sobbed, relieved that the razor wasn't meant for her, in horror of the self-mutilation playing out before her eyes. "Stop!"

His hand froze in mid-air. He blinked—looked at her—at the razorblade—at the blood. Charlie Blackhawk dropped the blade and sat down, staring at his own blood, mouth twitching. He didn't move as he watched the blood spurting from the open wounds. He seemed hypnotized by it. He was—*smiling*.

Sabrina's mind reeled. What horrible things had this mother done to drive her child mad? It was impossible for her to picture such atrocities, but she imagined as far as her twelve-year-old mind was willing to take her. She found herself thinking of puppies. Warm, furry puppies. Kids were like puppies, she thought, innocent and full of love. But if their rewards were kicks and beatings and abuse, then what?

(*Charlie was bleeding to death.*)

A tortured puppy grows into a mad dog, and a mad dog is dangerous and must be destroyed.

Charlie was whimpering.

Like a puppy?

(He will die and then I'll be free.)

Rambo would just blow it away with a grenade. There was no choice. All that remained was rage and wanting to be put out of its misery.

(He will die and I'll be free.)

Roboscout can do it, she told herself.

(And I'll be free.)

But this wasn't a movie.

And Charlie kept whining and giggling...and whimpering.

Something deep inside of Sabrina could not watch him die.

"Charlie!" He did not respond. "Damn you, snap out of it! Get the dishtowel. Do it now, Charlie."

Bewildered, he obeyed this new voice that was screaming somewhere in his head.

When he returned with the dishtowel she ordered him to untie her. He shook his head in distrust. "Let me stop the blood," she said calmly. "Or you will die."

Charlie fumbled with the ropes. It was difficult as he had little use of his wounded left hand. He untied her wrists, then her ankles. Sabrina rubbed away the pain, then took the towel from him and stood up. Her back ached, low and deep. She led him to the bathroom sink. (No more kitchens and dead things.) As she ran cold water over the ribbons of flesh, the sink filled with blood. She turned off the water and held the towel tightly over the wound, then applied pressure until the bleeding had subsided.

"Sit down on the toilet," she said. "Hold the towel in place and elevate your arm." He just looked at her. "Raise your damn arm and shut your eyes!" He did not understand but he did as she commanded. Quickly, she removed her slip and bound it tightly around his wrist.

He opened his eyes and spoke: "You still love me, don't you

Lucy Mae?"

"I'm tired, Charlie. I don't want to play games right now. Just keep holding your arm up and be quiet."

"Momma can't make me hurt you, see?" he said proudly, indicating his injured hand as though it offered proof.

Oh yes she can, Sabrina thought with despair. She looked at his crazy eyes and at that moment she wished with all her heart that she had let Charlie Blackhawk die.

CHAPTER TWENTY-SEVEN

Amy Hamill rested on the couch, propped up by big pillows. She relaxed as best she could. Her stomach was in a permanent knot and she was edgy. Afraid of the dreams. Ms. Flores was nice, but Amy feared that if she picked away too much at her insides that Flores would find out she was really crazy and they'd take her away again. Only this time they'd put her away in a place for crazy kids and she would never get out. She wondered if they had pink straight-jackets for little girls. And what did they do with the children when they got old? And did they let fathers visit? They didn't in the other place. So, she talked to Ms. Flores about safer things. It worked. Ms. Flores was pleased with her progress.

Amy was learning to keep things inside—but her stomach knotted and it was hard to keep her food down. She didn't want her father to know. She'd excuse herself from the table, run upstairs, vomit, brush her teeth, and come back down. She was losing more weight and felt like a melting ice cube, afraid that she'd soon disappear entirely.

Amy looked out the window and saw Freddy coming up the walk. She threw off the comforter and beat him to the door. He huffed and puffed his way up the front steps, smiling all the way. He held his school books under one arm and clutched the newspaper he'd picked up from the driveway. His face glowed from exertion and the joy of seeing his friend.

"Come on in."

"I miss you at school," he said, coming through the door and dropping his books in the entry. "I brought in your Dad's paper. Jeez Amy, you look aweful."

"I'm fine, really."

"Are you up for Monopoly?"

"You bet! Daddy's in his study. C'mon, we'll go ask him, but I'm sure it's okay."

Jerry smiled when they entered the room, glad to see his daughter's only friend.

"I brought your paper, Mr. Hamill. Can Amy play Monopoly?"

Jerry nodded, taking the paper from Freddy. He set the paper aside as he listened to the children climb the stairs. He picked up the paper, leaned back in his chair, and began reading. An insert fell to the floor, unnoticed.

* * * * * * *

Amy and Freddy sat on the floor of her bedroom, Monopoly board between them. Freddy was arranging stacks of money as Amy lined up the cards. They each rolled the dice.

"When are you coming back to school?" He asked. "It's no fun when you're not there."

Amy shifted her weight and took her turn. "Daddy says when I feel better. But Freddy, I don't think I'm ever going to feel better. Sometimes I feel like," she sighed, "like I'm dying."

Freddy didn't know what to say. His glasses slid down his nose and he pushed them up, nervously. "Don't ever say stuff like that. You're gonna get better."

She showed him the marks on her wrists. "I don't even remember how it happened—that's crazy, isn't it? And I can't stop dreaming about dead things—and the bad man—and the pretty girl. I'm crazy," she said with finality.

Freddy took his turn, landing on Park Place without buying it.

She knew he was letting her win.

* * * * * * *

It was nearly dark when Freddy left. Amy had won the game. It didn't bother her that he'd cheated in her favor. He didn't know how else to make her feel better. It meant that he cared. She walked down the hallway thinking about how much she'd miss Freddy when she died.

She entered her father's study. He looked worried. She would miss him too. As she neared him, she noticed the piece of paper that had fallen from the newspaper to the floor. She gazed at it, frozen, then looked at her father with astonishment. It was the insert that Meg Stinson had paid to have included in today's edition regarding her missing daughter.

Pointing at the photograph, she said, "That's the girl in my dreams, Daddy. She's real!"

* * * * * * *

The following morning Sabrina awoke to the rustling sounds of Charlie moving around in the cabin. He had removed her bonds. He no longer needed to keep her tied for he no longer slept. He just kept watching her. But the absence of ropes provided no sense of freedom for her. His eyes had become her prison. Her night had been restless. The aching deep in her back kept waking her, as did Charlie's muttering—and the memories of the razor blade and the madness.

There was no food and Sabrina felt weak. She rolled onto her side and moaned. Charlie saw movement and scurried to her. He sat on the bed, petting her face with his bandaged hand. She turned away and when she moved she felt a dampness, warm and unfamiliar.

Alarmed, Sabrina looked down—and saw.

She bolted upright, shoving Charlie's hand as she rose. "Shit," she was saying. "Oh shit oh shit oh shit!" She ran into the bathroom and slammed the door.

"Lucy Mae?"

"Leave me alone!"

The door was opening. "Get out!" she screamed, pushing her

weight against the door. "Get out, go away." Charlie yelped as the door knocked against his wounded hand. He pulled away, allowing her to slam the door, leaving him on the other side. "Damn it, stay out of here," she cursed, panic in her voice.

Sabrina leaned her back against the door and looked down. She cried. There was blood, everywhere blood—first Charlie's blood and now her own.

For the first time, Sabrina was menstruating.

Weighed down with defeat, she let her body collapse and slide down the length of the door. She pulled her knees up, hugging them tightly against her, head slumped forward.

She needed her mother. And she wanted Betty and Miss Cooney.

But Charlie Blackhawk stood beyond the door.

Why now? She wondered. Why here?

It just wasn't fair. Too many old movies, too many plot lines from Betty's romance novels. Nobody ever got their period in either one of them! "I am Roboscout," she said, feeling childish at saying the words. "Period or no period." Roboscout had kept her alive this long.

She pulled herself up and nervously removed her clothes. At any moment he might barge through the door. But she turned on the shower and got in, hoping he wouldn't pull open the curtain like Tony Perkins in Psycho. She looked into the drain and saw Janet Leigh's blank eye staring up at her in Hitchcockian black and white. The cold water numbed her and she washed herself quickly. Then she scrubbed her soiled undies as best she could. She dried herself with a soiled hand towel, then slipped back into the dirty uniform. She folded the towel and placed it between her legs, pulling the wet underwear over it to hold it in place. It felt like a soiled diaper, awkward and clumsy.

She was angry.

It was his fault.

Sabrina threw open the bathroom door and yelled at Charlie. He had to go to the store. They needed food. She needed Kotex. That was all there was to it. She refused to be embarrassed.

This was all his fault and he could damn well deal with it. She kept repeating her demands but he just kept pacing. She was screaming. He was holding his hands over his ears.

"I can't go where they know me," he said. "Not for that stuff."

"You have no choice. I need them. And with no food, we'll both die. Is that what you want?" A chill went through her—that was it—that was how the game would end. She pushed the thought from her mind.

Charlie was agitated as he stormed into the kitchen. "Devil's spawn!" he screamed. Sabrina heard the sounds of dishes smashing against the wall and wondered, if she ran for the door right now, if she could escape. "Shitdamn," he said. More glass breaking. She was within his sight and dared not move. "Kill the bitch, Charlie!" his Momma's voice demanded. Sabrina held her breath as he reentered the room.

"You're fucking everything up, Lucy," he said. "And you're trying to trick me again. If I gotta drive clear up to Arrowhead you think you'll have time to escape. Well, it ain't gonna work." Then in a near-whisper he added: "I'd kill you first."

And she believed him.

Had he said Arrowhead? I'm in the San Bernardino Mountains—cretin just told me so. "You can tie me up again, she said. "Or just take me with you...you know I'd never leave you, Charlie."

"Liar, liar, pants on fire," he sing-songed, reaching for the rope. First he bound her ankles, then tied her hands behind her back. His bandaged hand worked awkardly as he tightened the knots.

"It's cold in here, Charlie. Would you start a fire before you go?"

"Why should I?"

"Because you love me, Charlie." She used her best Lucy Mae voice, at first not understanding his rage. Then it hit her—he was upset because she was no longer a little girl. She had misplayed a very important rule of the game.

"And because I saved your life," she reminded him.

He slapped duct tape over her mouth.

"...don't gotta listen to you!"

But he started a fire before he left.

Sabrina began working the knots.

* * * * * * *

Jan Smith pumped up the volume in her earphones, creating her own lyrics to the tune that was playing: "Sunshine strangers on the road," she sang loudly and off-key. Her pink joggers added bounce to her step as she challenged the old dirt road. Mid-morning sunlight sifted through tree branches and powdered the ground.

Her cheeks were flushed. This was a beautiful day, her day off, and she was in party mode. Hawk hadn't come back to the General Store so she was seeking him out. He'll love it, she told herself—mature men love aggressive women. She wore a tight pink tee tucked into a denim mini-skirt and wore no bra or panties. She was ready to roll.

Walking along the road, she wondered what it would be like. He'd smile and invite her in. She imagined his hands removing her skirt...imagined the sex. When they finished she'd leave, not caring if he even remembered her name. Better he didn't. Just sunshine strangers getting it on, then moving on. Just how she liked it.

Jan was ready to have her itch scratched and hoped that she could find his cabin.

She reached the end of the road and the old wooden sign. She spun in a circle, looking in all directions, then spotted the chimney smoke just over the ridge. She sang as she ascended the steep hill that led to his cabin.

She knocked. No answer. She banged louder and waited, dancing to the song on her cassette player. No one came. She tried the door but it was locked, the window covered with newspaper. She turned off the player and walked around the cabin. The kitchen door was locked but she could see inside. Maybe this wasn't such a good idea, she thought. There was something about the room—the mess and the broken dishes. But what the hell, she'd come for a hot body not a cool housekeeper. Still, there was something unnerving about all that broken glass. It gnawed at her as she walked around the cabin and peered through a window into the shadowy room. Something moved. She squinted, peering through the dirty glass. He has a woman in there, she thought, then saw that it wasn't a woman but a child. She lay on the bed, tied with ropes, her mouth taped shut. Jan's heart pounded. Her instinct was to run. But the child looked back at her, pleadingly.

"Oh, my God," Jan said, beating her fists against the glass. "This is heavy shit."

* * * * * * *

Charlie Blackhawk heard the commotion the instant he turned off the engine. He cocked his head and listened. Then he slid cautiously from the car, leaving the door ajar so as not to make any noise, and swiftly and quietly climbed the hill.

Glass shattered as Jan broke the window. Charlie recognized her. The nosy little bitch from the General Store was invading his space—she'd find Lucy Mae! Outraged, Charlie lunged for her, grabbing her from behind. "Slut," he said, pulling her from the window. "Harlot!" He threw her, stunning her as her head hit the ground. He was on her before she could move. He giggled as his large hands squeezed tightly around her throat. As he strangled her, he slammed her head repeatedly against the ground. There were thuds, then a sickly crack like branches breaking. It was her skull. Her body fell limp, eyes staring up at the China blue sky and the tops of the swaying, whispering pines.

Her body twitched, then lay still.

Charlie tried to ignore his erection.

He picked up the dead girl and carried her to the back of the cabin, just outside the kitchen, tossing her carelessly to the ground. He got a shovel and started to dig.

Once the hole was dug, he walked over to the body and stood over it. So young, he thought, triggering memories of nights in the city.... "Whore, slut, harlot," he said. He sat on the ground and spoke to her. He reached beneath her skirt.

Jan Smith's sunshine stranger touched her in her dark and secret places, and promised not to tell.

* * * * * * *

Sabrina's form floated far beyond the cabin. It had been easy this time. She saw a sign that read: TO LAKE—an old car with the license plate HAWK—a dirt road leading to a tiny village. She saw an old wagon wheel in front of a building. She was frantic to escape. She'd seen Charlie grab the girl at the window. The game was very dangerous and the rules were changing. She looked around for anything that might tell her where she was. Anything at all. Buddy, Buddy, Buddy, she kept repeating. It made no sense. But nothing made sense anymore.

She heard Charlie's voice and instantaneously felt the mattress beneath her. He was naked when he entered the room, a cigarette dangling from his mouth, his eyes vacant. "Look, Momma," he said, gazing beyond Sabrina, unaware of her.

She watched as if hypnotized, unable to avert her stare. His body was covered in scars and burns, some old, some fresh. "The watching games," he snickered. He took a long drag from the cigarette, then removed it from his mouth.

His malignancy filled the room.

She moved her wrists against the slacking rope.

Smiling, Charlie lowered the hot ember to his naked flesh, to his scarred and disfigured penis.

Sabrina shut her eyes.

CHAPTER TWENTY-EIGHT

Meg Stinson watched as the dark blue BMW pulled into the driveway. The man had a child in the car, but he left her there as he got out and walked up to the house. He appeared harmless enough. When he had called she thought it was another crank call. She'd hung up. She couldn't understand the cruelty of people. There had been nine obscene phone calls already. But no one called with information on Sabrina, not until the odd call from the man named Jerry Hamill. After she'd hung up on him he called again, and kept calling until she was willing to listen. "She knows," he'd kept repeating, "My little girl knows."

Meg invited him in and they sat in the livingroom. "Tell me what you know about my daughter," she said. "You told me over the phone that you had information."

"I don't know where to begin. Little of this makes sense."

"Either you know something or you don't."

"My daughter has dreams."

"We all have dreams." Meg rose from the chair. "I think you'd better go now." She regretted letting this crackpot into her house. She should have just referred him to the police.

"Get out now" she said, pointing to the door.

He didn't move. "She has dreams about your daughter."

"About my daughter? Go on," she said, feeling compelled to listen.

Jerry told her about the dreams, the problems, the doctors. "I don't know why this is happening to her, but it's as if all this nonsense is starting to pull together and mean something. It's beyond logic—and I pride myself in being a logical man. I'm afraid for her, and I think you know...something."

The door opened. Meg turned and saw a tiny girl standing in the doorway, her eyes sunken, her body frail. She appeared to be seven or eight years old. Her unhealthy pallor was accentuated by pale, strawberry hair. Meg gazed at her with pity. The child was a stranger yet something about her was both familiar and unsettling.

"Amy," her father said.

"I know this house!" She ran through the room and into the front bedroom as Jerry and Meg followed. When they entered Sabrina's room Amy was beating her fists against the window. She turned, did a karate kick. "Roboscout!" she yelled. She pushed her way past them. As she neared the front door she stopped and turned. "Buddy," she whispered, then collapsed.

"Buddy." Meg repeated the name in disbelief as Jerry ran to his daughter.

"She knows what happened in this house," Meg was saying. "She knows about my Sabrina. Make her tell me!"

"Just shut up," he said, carrying Amy to the bedroom and placing her on the bed. "Get me a cold washcloth."

When Meg returned, Jerry was sitting on the bed soothing his daughter. Meg was touched by the gentleness in his voice, the kindness in his gestures. She handed him the cloth. Lovingly and tenderly, he wiped Amy's brow. "She'll sleep now," he said.

They returned to the livingroom. Jerry studied Meg, her eyes, her hair, her features—just as he'd studied the face on the flyer. He pulled the insert from his pocket and held it up, shaking it in Meg's face. "Tell me," he said. "You know—tell me."

"You have to wake her up," Meg said, ignoring him. "She has to tell us...."

"Look," he said, pointing to the photo. "I can see it, can't you?"

"See what?"

"You have the same face! You all have the same face! You're coloring, your features. Can't you see it?"

"What are you talking about?" She said, looking at the photo.

Jerry blurted out the words, knowing they sounded foolish, but convinced they were true. "My Amy was adopted. I'm certain Amy and your girl are sisters. That you're her birth mother."

"But that's absurd. Thousands of children are adopted. And don't you think I'd know?" Something stirred in the pit of her stomach, a memory that haunted her.

"Damn it, can't you see that both their lives are in danger? You owe us the truth."

"There's nothing to tell. What you're suggesting is impossible and I don't have to listen to you."

"They're in danger. Somehow, what's happening to your daughter is also affecting Amy. She's getting sicker. I need to understand what's happening. Look," he said, pointing to the flyer. "They even have the same birthday."

"Lots of people have the same birthday. Anyway, she can't be the same age. Just look at her. It's impossible."

Jerry sat down next to her. "She looks like you," he said softly. He put his arms around her, then buried her face against his shoulder. Instead of recoiling from his touch, Meg leaned into him. Why did this stranger make her feel so safe? Was it the gentleness he had shown with his daughter? The sincerity in his illogical words? There were things from her past that she shared with no one. Not even with Betty. But because of the situation she felt compelled to open up to this man that she'd known for less than fifteen minutes.

"She was dead," Meg said. "I know that she was dead." Secrets rose from their graves as she was being asked to confide them to this stranger. She hesitated. "I can't do this."

"I'm sorry, but right now the children are all that matter."

Meg began to speak, slowly at first. She told him how she'd run away with Junior and left nothing out. She couldn't look at him, but as she spoke a heavy weight was lifting from her. "You could never understand," she said. "I was sixteen and stupid and he turned me into garbage." She talked about the beatings, the prostitution, all of it. She told Jerry that she'd gotten pregnant and hoped that Junior would no longer want her—that he'd set her free.

Instead, he'd found men who'd pay top dollar for a pregnant whore—lots of them. "I was so young, so frightened, so beaten down. And he told me that when the baby came, he was going to sell it."

Jerry stroked her hair gently as she continued.

One day she and Junior had fought. He beat her again, worse this time. He threw her to the floor, kicking her repeatedly in the stomach before storming out of the motel room. "Later that night I went into labor," Meg said. "I was alone and terrified. He was going to sell my baby and there was nothing I could do. Where is my baby?" she cried. "Where is my Sabrina?"

"Shhh, it'll be alright," he said.

"It's never going to be alright! I'm never going to be forgiven, don't you see? My friend was taken from me. Sabrina was taken from me. It's my punishment, but how could I have known?"

"Known what?"

Meg continued, "The pain was terrible." Labor had been intense and quick and she gave birth alone, on the dirty bathroom floor. Sabrina was born—strong and healthy and loud. But the contractions didn't stop.

When the second baby came, she was tiny and blue and dead. It was as if, in the womb, Sabrina had hoarded all of her mother's nourishment. "Don't you see? She was dead. I'd stopped caring about myself long ago, but I had my baby now. I had to escape. Junior would never know there had been two of them, so I left the dead baby on the floor and I ran. I knew that she was dead so I ran away with my Sabrina in my arms."

"But the baby lived," Jerry said.

"I didn't know. I'm not a monster, I just didn't know."

"I know."

"I started building a new life, and slowly, I started feeling better about myself. But the past never goes away, does it?"

"What matters is that they need each other," Jerry said. Meg saw no judgment in his face nor did she hear blame in his voice.

"It's as if they've always been searching, reaching out to each other—as if they...." she paused.

"As if neither of them ever felt whole," he finished.

"My ex-wife and I had been trying to get pregnant for three years," Jerry volunteered. "Then one day an old friend from law school had the solution. A baby was available and I grabbed the opportunity. It didn't matter that it wasn't legal. He had connections and a birth certificate and other papers were forged and all was well with the world. I brought her home and my wife disliked her from the start. It ended up she had been on birth control pills the whole time. A baby was the last thing she wanted. Amy's fragility just made it more impossible for her to deal with. Amy was nothing more to her than a broken toy and an inconvenience. Things quickly deteriorated. She finally walked out and left me to raise Amy myself."

They held each other, sharing the silence.

* * * * * * *

Amy's sleep was restless. The girl was there again. "Buddy," the girl kept saying, but in the dream Amy knew that she was speaking to her. Pictures flashed like a frantic slide show. Darkness—trees—road signs—birds. The images held no meaning for Amy but the voice kept repeating, "Find me, find me, find me."

* * * * * * *

Outside it was nearly dark, but inside Meg Stinson's house the lights burned brightly. She sat with Jerry on the couch as Amy continued to sleep in the other room.

Amy was his angel, just as Sabrina was hers. Amy's health was poor from the start and her first year was spent in and out of hospitals. Later, other problems surfaced. It was difficult for

Meg to come to terms with the fact that the baby she'd left for dead was alive. It was a miracle.

"Amy is everything to me," he said.

"I know."

Jerry Hamill's sincerity moved her.

Amy entered the room, yawning and rubbing her eyes. Meg rose and knelt down before the child, looking into her face. "Amy, you know what happened in this house, don't you?"

"The bad man took the pretty girl."

"Who was he?"

"Dunno."

"Amy, where did he take her?"

"By the Christmas trees."

"Where are the Christmas trees?"

"Two lakes." She turned to her father. "I don't feel very good."

"Don't ask her any more questions. I think we should call the police."

"And tell them what? That a little girl had a dream? We have to find her before...." She put her hands firmly on Amy's shoulders. "Where are the lakes? Please, you have to tell me."

The corners of Amy's mouth turned down and her lip quivered. "The bad man yells."

"Leave her be," Jerry said.

"No, Daddy. We gotta find her."

* * * * * * *

Sabrina and Charlie sat at the kitchen table. He wore the same dirty jeans but a clean t-shirt and appeared unaware of the chill. Sabrina ate her cold meal. Charlie had brought supplies. Her period had ended as abruptly as it had begun and things were looking up. She didn't ask about the woman at the window. She didn't want to know.

"You tried to untie the ropes," he said.

"But you don't need them—see?"

"...just you and me, Lucy."

"Yes."

She stared at his face, distorted by the dim light of the candle. You think that I'm your prisoner, she thought, but I'm not. I'm smiling at you, but I'm watching old Miss Cooney eat an Oh Henry®. I'm not alone, not in my head. Meggie is here and Betty and you can't control that. They're here, inside of me, all the time.

"Thank you, Lucy," he said.

"For what?"

"For coming back. It was so empty out there without you." He reached for her hand across the table. "I never stopped looking, I never stopped missing you."

"I'm here now."

"And see? I haven't hurt you, have I? I even threw away the packrat. I been good to you, treated you nice and everything." He sighed, looking at her pleadingly. "Maybe now you can...." But his voice drifted into silence.

"I can what, Charlie?"

But he was gone again, staring into the candleflame. Twitching. He didn't blink. His breathing was shallow. She thought she saw a tear on his face, but it could have been a trick of the light.

It didn't matter.

She took another bite of her sandwich. When this happens to him, he goes somewhere else, she thought, and it's not happy there. When I close my eyes, when I try real hard, I float away, beyond this place and I'm free. I am free and he is in a prison.

The rules of his game still eluded her. It was strange. Bizarre. He wanted his sister, she knew that much. He promised not to hurt her, but she knew when Momma's voice came that the rules shifted. That's why he kept hurting himself—so he wouldn't hurt her. But he could. It was creepy. And there was something else she couldn't figure out. (Can I what, Charlie?)

Something important.

She pushed away from the table, broken glass scrunching beneath her slippers. Charlie cocked his head. As hard as she tried to think like him, insanity gave him the edge. As soon as she thought she'd nailed it, something in his head would shift, exposing another layer of madness, and she'd have to start over.

She hated him.

One wrong move, one wrong word and it would be over.

She could feel his eyes watching her, holding her as tightly as any rope. Her hands felt cold. She shoved them into her pockets. Her fingers felt something—something she'd forgotten was there.

Her hand closed around the small Girl Scout knife.

* * * * * * *

"There's just too many lakes," Jerry said, looking at the atlas. "There's Castaic, that's close to here."

"So's Lake Hollywood, but there's no Christmas trees," she said.

"What?"

"Amy said Christmas trees. The lakes around here are warm as bath water and surrounded by scrub. I think we should be looking for mountain lakes.

"Trees. Two lakes," Amy said absently. She was sitting between them looking at the sketches pinned to the refrigerator. "You're an artist," she said with admiration.

Meg reached out and stroked her hair. "You're a beautiful child." Amy smiled sweetly, then turned her attention back to the drawings.

Jerry slammed his fist on the table. "There's lakes everywhere! We don't even know if they're in California. They could be in Oregon or Washington. Or anywhere. I don't know where to start."

"California. We have to start someplace. Mountains—Santa Monica, Angeles Crest. There's Frazier Park—I know there's trees there. God Jerry, there's so many. There's the Sierras, the San Bernardino's."

"Yes, the Sam Berdino's," Amy said.

"Amy, are you certain?"

"I think so. I think I heard that name...but I'm not sure. I'm scared, Daddy. We gotta find her quick."

"Please God, help my baby."

"Meg," said Jerry, "do you have any road maps?"

"I think Betty might." She stopped. Her voice choked as she continued. "There might be some in the night stand in the other bedroom...I still can't go in there."

Jerry returned with several folded maps, tossing them on the table. "Bingo," Meg said, waving the San Bernardino map. Jerry unfolded it. "Well, there's certainly trees and lakes, lots of them."

"Look for two lakes close together—or Twin Lakes, something like that."

"Hawk," Amy said.

"Hawk Lake, Twin Lakes, two lakes. Damn it Jerry, it's got to be there. Look!"

"That's not helping," he said calmly.

Amy put her arms around Meg and hugged her. "It's okay," she said. She was as frightened as Meg. If only she'd paid closer attention to the dreams. If only she'd known they were important. Finding the girl, Sabrina, was up to her. They were depending on her and she was scared. "Don't worry, we'll find her."

Meg burst into tears.

"...Crestline," Jerry said. "Big Bear, Green Lake...."

"It's hopeless," Meg sobbed.

"...Deep Creek, Running Springs, Arrowhead...."

Amy gasped.

"All the way to Arrowhead," she whispered.

CHAPTER TWENTY-NINE

Charlie descended deeper and deeper into the bowels of madness, incapable of back tracking to even a flash of lucidity. The deeper he sank into the darkness, the more frightened Sabrina was. He no longer ate. He no longer slept. One moment he was quiet as death, the next babbling and incoherent.

And there was the rabid, endless pacing.

And the screams...and Momma's shrill voice...and the tears. It was unnerving, watching this big, strong man sob like a baby. She didn't know what to make of it all. Just when she'd think she had a handle on things—that she could calm his rages—everything would turn upside-down again.

During one of his rants she'd recovered her knife, unnoticed, and had slipped it back into her pocket.

But the game was impossible when the rules kept changing.

Sabrina looked at her hands and wondered if they could kill—if that was what really made one brave in this world—if that was what she'd need to do to survive this asylum. It looked so easy in the movies, but this was real. A sick, empty feeling stirred inside of her.

The birds were silent.

She looked up.

Charlie had stopped pacing.

* * * * * * *

Jerry Hamill pulled off his tie and threw it on the dashboard.

They should have started out earlier, he knew that now. It was his own fault and Meg was frantic. She'd wanted to start out last night—right away—but he'd convinced her to wait until morning. Their search would have been futile in the dark. It seemed an impossible enough task in daylight. After a restless night, they hit the road at 5:30 am. It should've easily been a two hour drive from Los Angeles, but this wasn't the weekend. Jerry hadn't calculated work-day traffic and it was taking far longer.

Meg was unable to sit still in the seat next to him, constantly shifting her weight and checking the map.

It was daylight when the BMW began its ascent up the steep mountain road.

"Look at all the Christmas trees," Amy said from where she sat in the back seat. She was laughing. "These are the trees." The sun burned away the early morning mists and they saw pine trees everywhere.

When they got to Running Springs, Jerry saw the road sign pointing the direction to Arrowhead. He hung a left. The BMW climbed the twisting mountain road, through vacillating sunlight, through shadows of towering pines, toward their destination. He prayed they were on the right track.

"Arrowhead," Amy said, hope in her voice.

Jerry looked over at Meg and wondered what would happen to her if they couldn't find Sabrina—or if they were too late. He knew, that in him, she had recruited the most unlikely of saviors—a man who lived in his head—a man whose greatest adventures were played out in law libraries. He was no hero, he knew, but he also knew that he must find Sabrina—for his daughter—for Meg. And the urgency propelled him onward.

Meg was at her breaking point. She was tense, her features drawn. She fidgeted and hyperventilated. Even little Amy showed more pluck—Meg's courage was tenuous at best.

"It's alright, Meg," he kept repeating. "We're going to find her." But his words were of little comfort.

* * * * * * *

"I wanna watch, you rotten little bastard! Do you hear me?"
His Momma's voice pierced the air like an icepick.

"Good little boys mind their Momma's!"

Sabrina cringed. He was pacing again. He swung his arms stiffly from side to side, and with each motion the makeshift bandage loosened from his wounded hand. He clenched his hands into fists and held them over his ears. He moaned, and the moan became a growl, the growl a roar. Momma's poison burned through his brain.

Charlie opened his mouth and detonated an explosion of screams.

Sabrina bolted upright and ran into the bathroom, slamming the door. She pushed her back against the door and gasped for breath. The heavy pounding of her heart reverberated throughout her body.

This was the most frightening episode yet.

She shook.

"God says you better fucking mind your Momma!"

Then silence.

Scary silence.

Sabrina did not move...she did not breathe.

* * * * * * *

"Only six more miles," Jerry said, glancing at the odometer.

"Hurry, Daddy—she's scared."

Meg covered her face with her hands. "We're never going to find her."

"Damn it, you have to have hope. Hope is all we're running on and we need all we can muster."

"We'll find her," Amy said. Her thin fingers reached forward from the back seat and touched Meg on the shoulder.

Meg covered Amy's hand with her own.

CHAPTER THIRTY

Charlie slammed his body full weight against the door. Once. Twice. The force threw Sabrina across the room. Hinges tore loose. Wood splinters flew through the air as the crippled door swung inward and crashed top first into the shower stall.

Sabrina spun around.

Charlie filled the doorway, arms upraised, hands gripping the door frame like a demented Sampson, chest heaving.

She was trapped. There was no means of escape. The small bathroom shrunk around her. Charlie's form loomed like a giant in the narrow doorway. The window was too small—she knew that. The door where Charlie stood was the only way out.

But he blocked the exit.

Panting, giggling, eyes glazed.

He held no weapon.

He didn't need one.

He was a giant and she was twelve years old.

She was trapped. She didn't want to die. She had to do something.

Anything.

"Roboscout!" she yelled, charging straight at Charlie. Startled, caught off guard, it took a split second for his brain to send the message to his body. He started to lower his arm. To grab at her. But it was too late. She was too fast. She dodged to the side—dove under his arm before his hand could reach her. She yelled again as she ducked past him—"ROBOSCOUT!"— and raced into the other room, aiming for the kitchen.

Charlie spun around, his long arms stretching toward her. He grabbed her from behind; stopping her in her tracks.

Sabrina flew through the air, onto her back, across the mattress.

"Cretin! Bastard!"

She looked up, into his maniacal, watery eyes.

Death looked back at her.

Not now, her mind screamed, not like this.

Her right hand reached into her pocket.

"Momma says," he was saying as he slid across the mattress next to her. He cocked his head sideways. "Listen," he said. "Can you hear?"

"No! She's not here, Charlie. Don't listen. Don't...."

But he moved closer.

And he was smiling.

Her heart pounded.

Her body froze.

His bandaged hand reached toward her. The reek of infection permeated the space between them, making her gag. Then, his fingers touched her.

There was no time to think.

The sharp blade of the Girl Scout knife plunged downward, through the bandage, into his festering wound.

Amy gasped.

Charlie shrieked.

He bolted from the bed and grabbed his wrist—raised his hand above his head and looked up.

At the seeping blood.

At the offering.

He shrieked again—tore off the bandage—stared at his ribboned, rotting flesh—at the fresh stab wound.

He stood between Sabrina and the kitchen door. Between Sabrina and escape. Between life and death.

He was sobbing again.

Like a child.

Knife in hand, Sabrina ran into the kitchen and through the

shards of broken glass.

To the door.

She reached for the handle.

The sounds of scrunch, scrunch, scrunching across the floor behind her.

Coming closer.

Closer.

Charlie grabbed the hand which held the knife and squeezed her wrist.

"Drop it."

"No."

He squeezed harder.

"NO!"

Maintaining a tight grip around her wrist, his other hand went for the knife. Slowly, one by one, Charlie peeled away her fingers.

It clattered to the floor.

Sabrina kicked at the knife.

Missed.

He leaned down. Picked it up. Faced her.

"He has a knife!" Amy yelled from the back seat.

Meg burst into tears. "We're too late. Oh God, why? Why, my Sabrina?"

* * * * * * *

Jerry's foot pressed down on the accelerator. Tires screeched around the sharp curves. The car swayed back and forth across the center line, barely missing an oncoming van. Jerry refused to believe that it was too late. If Sabrina died, what would happen to Amy? But he knew. The bond between them was too strong—one could not survive without the other.

Up the two-lane road, past a sign which read: Pine Lake, elevation 6,400 feet, and straight through a stop sign.

Jerry knew that if he could save Sabrina he would save his precious Amy as well.

"I know that thing," Amy said, pointing off to the right, to an old wagon wheel leaning against a building. "Daddy, stop! I know that thing."

But he was going too fast.

He took his foot off the gas, allowing the car to slow down some before applying the brakes.

"Daddy, go back. I knew that."

Jerry u-turned, then stepped on the gas. The BMW's speed-ometer shot upward.

"On your side, Daddy. Over there."

Jerry lifted his foot from the gas pedal and jerked the steering wheel to the left. "Hang on!" he said—hitting the brake. The car skidded off the road and into the graveled parking lot. He slammed the brake pedal to the floor.

Gravel flew. The car spun.

Once. Twice.

Tilted over onto two wheels as they careened across the lot.

The BMW slammed against the wagon wheel, then into the corner of the building, thudding down on all four tires.

Clouds of dust swirled around the car. A broken wagon wheel spoke sailed through the air, then crashed down onto the hood of his car. He looked around to make sure Amy and Meg were unhurt, then unsnapped his seatbelt.

"The knife," Amy said.

Jerry bolted from the car and raced toward the building.

* * * * * * *

Charlie pushed Sabrina against the wall, to the left of the kitchen door. He held her there and looked at the knife which he held in his right hand.

"You promised, Charlie."

He looked down at her. At her pretty green uniform. At her pleading eyes.

"You promised not to hurt me, remember?"

He appeared puzzled, as if he didn't know who she was.

Sabrina looked straight into his frozen gray eyes. "It's me, Charlie. It's your Lucy Mae. It's Lucy."

"...won't hurt you ever again."

"That's right, Charlie. You promised," she said calmly, but her heart was pounding.

Charlie's attention was drifting from her.

He twitched.

Charlie didn't want to bother Lucy. She was still sick and breathing oddly, but Charlie knew that he had to mind his Momma. It was in the bible—she'd said so—over and over.

But he was smarter than Momma.

The first night that it had happened, the first night that she had made him, he'd made Lucy Mae cry. He was determined not to make her cry again. Never. No matter what Momma said—no matter what Reverend Church said on the radio—no matter what God said...no matter how much it aroused him.

He loved his little sister. So he and Momma would come into her room and he would crawl into her bed and he would whisper secrets to her. Then, to distract Momma, Charlie would do things to himself—with cigarettes or razors or pliers—all the while whispering his pleas to Lucy.

But she never answered.

That last night, Charlie crawled into his sister's bed, certain that tonight would be the night she would forgive him.

"Get to it," Momma demanded from across the room.

"I love you, Lucy," he whispered. "Forgive me."

But she didn't answer.

She didn't move.

Lucy Mae was dead.

He bolted from the bed, screaming.

"You drunken, rotten bitch! You've killed my Lucy. I told you she was sick. Couldn't you hear her coughing? I told you she was making funny noises when she breathed. Why didn't you take her to the doctor? Why? Why? I told you to. I begged!"

Momma took a step backwards, then went out of the room.

Charlie followed, as Reverend Churchill's voice blasted from the radio. He grabbed the radio from the shelf, smashing it onto the floor. It broke into a million pieces and silenced the good Reverend forever. Then he turned to Momma as she cowered against the wall.

He was young, barely thirteen, but his rage made him strong.

He grabbed her by the neck, pushing his thumbs hard against her throat. Something went pop, but he kept on squeezing until her body went limp. He let her drop to the floor.

He'd silenced her forever, too.

That was the night Charlie Blackhawk sent his mother to heaven.

His maddened pleas filled the night as he held Lucy, but she never answered.

Never said the one thing he needed to hear.

The next morning he walked out the door and never looked back.

"Can't make me," he said. "Can't make me hurt you." But his hand kept rising.

Sabrina held her breath.

The game was totally out of control.

Tears welled in his eyes as he looked down at her. "I love you, Lucy," he said.

Then the knife plunged downward—

Sabrina screamed—and Charlie thrust the knife into his own abdomen.

He didn't react as it stabbed over and over again, through his t-shirt and deep into his flesh—did not register the pain, just kept stabbing.

"Can't make me hurt you," he kept saying.

He pulled out the knife, grabbed it with both hands, began stabbing himself again.

"See?" He said.

He was smiling.

"See see see?" He chanted the word like a mantra as he slashed at his stomach, his groin.

"No Charlie oh God no," Sabrina moaned. "No Charlie stop."

Raising the knife, he said, "You can't ever leave me again."

Sabrina turned, grabbing at the doorknob.

She pulled the door open as the knife sliced through the air over her head, and ran out.

She leaped over the back step and onto the ground and took off running—over a mound of freshly turned soil. Her foot tripped over something—

a rock?

Her blue slipper flew from her foot and she sprawled, face first, onto the ground.

Charlie's voice was ranting from the kitchen. "I won't hurt you Lucy not ever again I dropped the knife see? see? see? you can't leave me now I love you Lucy you promised you can't ever leave me again I need you I need you to..."

Sabrina pulled herself to her feet and turned to retrieve her slipper.

That was when she saw something jutting out from the mound of dirt.

It wasn't a rock.

It was a hand.

Posed as if it were trying to hitch a ride—the fingernails were painted bright pink—it was the woman from the window.

"...can't leave me Lucy gotta forgive me gotta gotta gotta...." His voice was getting closer.

Sabrina turned and ran.

She heard screams.

But she couldn't tell if they were coming from Charlie or from herself.

CHAPTER THIRTY-ONE

Jerry propelled himself through the front door of the Wagon Wheel. Breakfast customers were clustered at the window to his far left, pointing at the BMW where it had crashed into the building. They shook their heads and muttered, then turned their attention to him.

"Where are the two lakes?" Jerry asked.

They stared at him as though he were an alien who had just crashed his saucer.

"The two lakes," he repeated. "Where are the two lakes?"

A tall man, coffee pot in hand, eyed Jerry angrily. Stitched on the front of his stained apron, in brown letters, was the name Gus. What remained of his hair was white and bushed out above his large ears. "Yer gonna pay for that," he said.

"Where are the two lakes!"

A waitress with dyed black hair answered him from where she stood behind the counter. Arrowhead's up the road a ways." She chewed on her gum, snapping it loudly, eying him.

"Then there's Big Bear the other way—a couple small ones in between."

"Are there any near here?"

"Pine Lake, of course," Gus said, as if responding to the village idiot. "That old wagon wheel was over a hundred years old. Yer gonna pay for it."

"Where is it? How do I get there?"

There was no answer. Jerry threw up his arms, turned to the door, then back again. "It's important."

The waitress snapped her gum again and yawned. "The dirt road," she said, pointing out the window.

"Lake ain't much bigger'n a puddle of warm piss," someone said.

A bell tinkled overhead as Jerry opened the door. Halfway through the door he spun around and addressed Gus: "Call the sheriff—the Highway Patrol—whatever it is you've got around here!"

"You bet your sweet ass I will. You're gonna pay...."

But Jerry was gone.

"Goddam crazy city bastard," Gus said.

And reached for the phone.

* * * * * * *

All four tires left the ground as the car flew over a deep rut in the dirt road. Jerry slammed on the brakes, trying to avoid the parked car directly in his path.

"Hawk!" Meg said, pointing to the license plate.

The BMW came to an abrupt halt, hitting the back bumper of the old Nova.

The engine jerked and died.

"Look at the sign, Jerry. It wasn't two lakes—it was TO LAKE. Hawk—to lake—thank you, Amy—thank you, thank you, thank you." Meg was crying again.

"The girl is close," Amy said.

"Where?"

Then they heard the scream.

* * * * * * *

Sabrina scrambled away from the cabin, past the Ponderosa pine, toward the open space. She could hear Charlie gaining on her—feel his breath panting behind her. "Don't leave me."

She ran faster.

She felt him grab her legs.

She lost her balance—fell to the ground—twisted around to face him.

He was hugging her leg and sobbing, covered in his own blood, covering her with his blood. His voice was weak.

"Please," he said.

Sabrina heard a yell and looked up. She saw a man racing in their direction, running straight at Charlie. He was charging at them like Rambo. No, like Chuck Norris. Like a hero. But instead of wearing camouflage he was wearing a suit and his only weapon was the rock which he held in his hand.

Sabrina watched in awe as the man sailed through the air and landed, half on Charlie, half on the ground. The impact threw Charlie onto his back. The man raised his arm and slammed the rock downward, grazing Charlie's head.

"Don't leave me," Charlie whimpered.

Again, the rock slammed down, this time full force against Charlie's skull.

More blood.

More whimpering.

Visions of abused puppies and mad dogs raced through Sabrina's brain.

Again, the rock hit its mark with a loud cracking sound.

"Lucy...."

"Stop," Sabrina said, her arm reaching toward her rescuer. "Stop. He's dying—he's already dying! Please stop."

The man's arm froze in mid-air. He looked at Charlie—at Sabrina—at the bloodied rock which he held.

"Please stop," she repeated.

Something rattled from deep inside Charlie's chest.

"Don't leave me," he said.

"I'll never leave you, Charlie."

He curled his large body into a fetal position—rested his head upon her lap.

"This time I saved you, didn't I, Lucy?" Charlie said. The deranged man's voice had become that of a tormented child.

"Yes, Charlie. This time you saved me."

His breathing was shallow.

He smiled up at her with the innocence of a little boy.

As he drifted towards death, there were visions swimming in his head.

"I'll never leave you, Charlie," Lucy Mae said.

She stood before Charlie, smiling at him. He saw that she was wearing her Girl Scout uniform but it was the most brilliant white he had ever seen, as white as the shimmering light that surrounded her.

"I love you," he said.

Her arms were outstretched, reaching out to him.

"Forgive me."

"I forgive you, Charlie." She motioned to him. "Come," she said.

Charlie reached out and took her hand and she led him into the pure white light.

Charlie Blackhawk closed his eyes.

"I forgive you," Sabrina said, finally understanding the purpose of the game, finally giving him the words he needed to hear.

She eased out from under him, lowering his head gently to the ground. The man in the suit stood over her, looking more like a CPA than a hero. But he was a hero. A real live hero. She reached up and took his hand. He pulled her to her feet. Sabrina walked with him, then stopped, pulling her hand from his.

She walked back to where Charlie lay. She pulled off her sweater as she spoke to his lifeless form. "I know you couldn't have killed me, Charlie." She covered him with the green sweater he had given her on her birthday, then walked away.

She knew, that in the instant it had taken Charlie to push his way through the bathroom door, that she was capable of killing him. It had nothing to do with right or wrong—strength or weakness—or even hatred.

It had to do with the will to survive.

And Sabrina was a survivor.

She felt the warm sun against her skin—heard the birds

singing—inhaled the fresh mountain air.

She was free.

The game was over.

In some strange and twisted way, they had both won.

The sound of a police siren echoed through the mountains.

Again, the man in the suit held out his hand to her. She put her hand in his as they descended the hill and walked toward the car.

Her rescuer. Her hero.

* * * * * * *

"They're safe," Meg said, squeezing Amy's hand.

The nightmare was over.

Amy watched as her father came down the hill. The girl was with him and when she saw Amy she ran toward her, auburn hair flowing in her wake. Just like in the dream. Amy ran to her. They stopped—faced each other.

The sound of the police siren was getting closer.

Amy's hand reached out, her small fingers tracing Sabrina's features—her nose, her brow. Amy looked into her jade green eyes and smiled. This was the girl with the crocuses—the girl who spoke to her in dreams—the girl in the photograph.

And she was real.

"Buddy," Sabrina said. "My wonderful, wonderful Buddy." She threw her arms around Amy and held her tight.

The girls laughed and cried and spun in circles, mirroring each others every movement as if in a perfectly choreographed dance.

"You're real," they said simultaneously, then laughed.

Amy felt contentment as Sabrina held her. It was just as it had been in the happy dream—as if she'd always been nothing more than a broken fragment and was finally whole.

Whole and strong.

EPILOGUE

Charlie Blackhawk's body was taken to the County Morgue. The tag on his toe read: JOHN DOE. The authorities had come up with nothing that shed any light on the man named Charlie Blackhawk. He didn't exist.

They found several ID's in his car, none of them his. They all belonged to unsolved cases scattered throughout the country.

His driver's license was a fake.

He had no Social Security number.

No one seemed to have known him or knew where he came from.

They ran his fingerprints through the computer and came up empty.

All he had was a name and they'd assumed even that wasn't real.

He was a dead-end.

So he lay in a cold, dark drawer. Unclaimed. In death, as in life, Charlie Blackhawk had managed to remain The Invisible Man. Just how he liked it.

* * * * * * *

It was autumn in Hidden Meadows. The leaves were turning yellow and brown and orange. They drifted like kites, then fluttered downward, blending their autumn palette on lawns and in gutters.

Three children sat on the lawn in front of the Colonial house.

Amy wore the locket Freddy had given her for her birthday. Inside it were photographs of Sabrina and herself. A large cardboard box sat on the ground between Amy and Freddy. They both reached into the box and handed Sabrina more crocus bulbs.

The three children laughed.

Sabrina dug holes with a spade and planted the bulbs, covering them with soil and patting down the dirt. Then she held out her hand for more.

Amy was gaining weight. The bad dreams were gone. The children at school no longer teased her. Or Freddy. They knew that if they did, they'd have Sabrina to contend with—and nobody wanted to mess with Sabrina. Sabrina was her twin, her sister, her best friend. And Sabrina was popular.

Amy looked back at the house. Meg and her father stood at the window. Meg held an artist's brush in her hand. Her father had his arm around her and they were waving.

Amy waved back.

They had kept their promise.

Amy and Sabrina were together.

Amy smiled as she remembered their long flight to Connecticut—she and Sabrina meeting their grandmother.

They were a real family.

And every Saturday their mother and father drove them into Hollywood to visit with old Miss Cooney. She was like family, too.

Amy reached into the box and handed her sister another bulb.

Come next spring, at 11 Avenida Larkspur, hundreds of crocuses would push their way through the soil in a rainbow of color. White and blue and purple and yellow.

Sabrina's crocuses.

Flowers bursting forth with promise—promises fulfilled—and promises for tomorrow.

"There are only two lasting bequests we can hope to give our children. One of these is roots; the other, wings."

—Hodding Carter

ABOUT THE AUTHOR

LONNI LEES has had several of her short stories published in *Hardboiled Magazine*, where she is a regular contributor. Her stories have also appeared in the e-zines *Yellow Mama* and *Einstein's Pocket Watch*, as well as in the anthology, *Deadly Dames*. Stories will be appearing shortly in the anthologies, *Whodunit?* and *Battling Boxers*.

She has won awards for her writing as well as her art. In the past she did illustrations for books and for the *L.A. Mensa Journal*. Her artwork had accompanied several stories by other writers in *Yellow Mama* and *Black Petals*.

Lonni was twice selected as a Writer-in-Residence at Hedgebrook, a writers' retreat for women on Whidbey Island in Washington State. She's traveled to many countries, and lived in several states; and currently resides in Tuscon, Arizona, with her scientist husband, Jonathan. She often shows her art at a Tuscon gallery. She's currently working on another novel, and on a collection of stories with her sister, Arlette Lees.